THE JEWELS OF CLEOPATRA

Iain McLaughlin and Claire Bartlett

Erimem: The Jewels of Cleopatra © Iain McLaughlin and Claire Blartlett
Editor: Julianne Todd
Range Editor: Iain McLaughlin
First published in 2020
Erimem and associated concepts Copyright © 2020 Iain McLaughlin
All rights reserved.
Cover illustration by Dorina Petco
No part of this publication may be reproduced, stored in a retrieval system or
transmitted in any form or by any means, electronic, mechanical, photocopying,
recording or any other manner without prior written permission of the copyright
holder.
First published in 2020 by Thebes Publishing
follow us online:
www.thebespublishing.com
https://www.facebook.com/ThebesPublishing
https://twitter.com/ThebesNews
ISBN: 978-1-910868-37-9

THEBES PUBLISHING

ERIMEM

THE JEWELS OF CLEOPATRA

STONE

Louie Spironi was born stupid.

It was unlucky that not only was Louie stupid, he was too stupid to actually know he was stupid.

Louie had been born in 1914, the day after war was declared in Europe. I guess the two things weren't connected. He was the product of a union between his father, a surly bum of a docker who turned pretty readily to violence when he'd taken a drink, and an actress who turned to prostitution when she couldn't find a job in the theatre or in the moving pictures. Unfortunately she was a poor actress and spent more of her time on her back than on the stage.

When Louie's mother found out that she was pregnant she selected the most likely candidate from the possibilities and with her four brothers, she made Louie's "father" do the right thing. Doing the wrong thing would have led to his legs coming off second best against pick-axe handles.

It turned out that Louie's mother, Elsie, had made a poor choice of father. Rico Spironi hated his possible son and hated his wife for inflicting marriage and parenthood on him. He took his revenge regularly, putting her in hospital several times before a clubbing blow on Louie's ninth birthday sent Elsie to the floor by way of striking her head on a table. She died two days later in hospital. Rico died at the end of a hangman's rope in Folsom State Prison two months later. He was still recovering from the beating Elsie's brothers had dished out when they hung him.

None of his uncles wanted young Louie, so he was taken into

the care of a Catholic orphanage. He was stupid enough to miss his psychotic "father". For a while at least. In the orphanage Louie fell under the spell of the worst influences there – worse even than the priests. He was part of the gang that dominated the orphanage. Admittedly he was the one in the gang that the rest made fun of, but at least he was *in* the gang.

When the state and the priests sighed with relief and threw Louie out onto the streets on his sixteenth birthday, Louie did the only thing he knew how to do – he turned to crime. He found the older boys who had been in the orphanage gang and had been thrown out before him. He followed their lead in joining Benny Archer's gang. In 1933, when Benny suffered what was noted in police reports as an "accidental death by suicide" – he accidentally stabbed himself seventeen times before shooting himself in the back of the head twice – Louie joined the rival Peterman outfit.

For the remainder of the 1930s, Louie worked as a low-level hood for Peterman. He wasn't smart enough to earn a quick promotion. That also meant he wasn't smart enough to be in danger of becoming a rival for the boss.

Louie did okay for himself. He wore nice suits and he made good money – and in the hard days of the 1930s not many could say that. The money meant that he had lots of girls. When people are starving they don't mind the conversation at dinner being dull, and a full belly helped the girls forget how Louie expected to be rewarded. By the latter years of the 1930s, Louie had a regular girl, Carmen. Okay, so she was a prostitute, but hey, his mother had been a whore. What was the big deal? She was classy. She only worked the top level guys – the union bosses, the councilmen, the guys who had businesses. She only worked when the boss wanted information from these guys. She was more of a spy than a whore. When she wasn't working the boss was happy for her to see Louie. He knew Louie would look after her. When she stopped working they'd get married. He would still visit his other whores but he would make sure Carmen never found out he cheated. She didn't deserve to be humiliated by knowing.

In 1939, Louie had eventually gained a sort of promotion. Normally the progress through the ranks was for one of the boys to become second or third in command of enforcement in a district or on a street and work up to running that area. Louie didn't have the brains for that. He did have the stomach for the most appalling violence, though. There was no skill or subtlety in his work. He broke bones, sheared fingers off, applied blowtorches to the soles of feet and took his Bowie knife to the flesh of anyone he was told to. Louie's promotion was to become the head enforcer of the Peterman organisation. He proved his worth by crucifying a priest who had marched into Mr Peterman's office and demanded that he stop taking protection money from the businesses around the church. Louie had taken the job of hammering the nails into the wrists and ankles himself. He was surprised that the statues were all wrong when they showed the nails through Christ's palms. He had been interested to feel the nails scrape past the bones. A lot of the guys in Louie's are of expertise had signatures. Jimmy the Smile had got his name by carving a victim's mouth into an ear to ear smile. Fingers picked up his nickname by collecting the fingers of men he tortured. Miss Lacy was the worst of the bunch. It was rare for women to be tortured but when they were, it was Miss Lacy who did it. Nobody knew her real name but they all knew that she kept the underwear of her victims as a memento of her work. It was known that Miss Lacy liked women. And that she liked hurting them more. Louie didn't get a nickname. He was just Louie.

The promotion meant that Louie moved to a nice apartment in a decent neighbourhood. He was able to have Carmen stay over. There were days Louie didn't have to work. If those coincided with one of Carmen's days off they could spend the whole days together.

Louie was too stupid to see that behind Carmen's beautiful, painted-on face, her eyes were dead. Years of self-loathing and shame had killed the life they had once had. Louie didn't notice. He was too busy watching her ass.

For a stupid man given a hellish start in life, Louie Spironi had fallen into a very comfortable life.

But in late 1940, Louie Spironi did the stupidest thing he had ever done in his life.

In November 1940, Louie Spironi got involved in throwing

his weight behind a real nasty bit of business being carried out by some of Mr Peterman's men.

On a warm November morning, Louie Spironi was stupid enough to pick a fight with Erimem.

ANDY

Adam Docherty squinted and looked around. He pushed up the brim of his fedora and took in the surroundings. Poor schmuck, he was still getting used to being a time traveller. And, yes, I will be using words like "schmuck" a lot. This was the 1940s, kid. Get used to it.

'It's really Hollywood,' Adam said. 'I mean, it's *really Hollywood*.'

Erimem adjusted her own wide-brimmed hat to a stylish angle. 'Yes,' she said patiently. 'It is really Hollywood.' That hat really went with the two piece she was wearing. She genuinely looked like a movie star. Which is fair enough I suppose, but we'll get to that in a minute.

Addam was still looking around, taking in the street, the old cars, the kitsch store fronts. There was no way to deny where and when we were. 'But it's 1940,' he said. 'We're in Hollywood in 1940.'

Ibrahim patted Adam on the shoulder sympathetically. 'You'll get used to it.'

'Oh, my gosh.' A middle-aged broad (I will also be using "broad" if I feel like it. If you don't like it, bite me.)

Erimem looked at the middle aged woman and gave a friendly smile. 'Are you all right?'

The old broad didn't hear the question. 'It's you,' she said.

Okay. Erimem was a bit bemused by that but tried not to show it. 'Yes.'

'It's *you*,' the woman repeated. 'You're the "Warrior Queen of the Nile" girl.'

You could hear the confusion in Adam's voice. 'How do they…'

The old broad delivered the answer. 'We saw your movie.'

She wasn't alone. She had a guy – a husband, I guessed, and a couple of kids who looked straight out of Stepford. They were the embodiment of children being seen and not heard – and frankly I wasn't even all that keen on seeing them. It was the husband who spoke. 'We've seen all your movies.'

That confused his wife. 'I thought she'd only done one.'

The manic star-struck look didn't move from the husband's face, even though he'd been caught out. 'But we saw it lots of times.'

The broad had to back her husband up. 'Oh, yeah, we did. For sure.'

This was when we worked out that we hadn't filled Adam in completely on our interest in 1940 Hollywood. 'You made a film?' He was a bit surprised. I would say "agog" but it's a silly word, so I won't.

The woman – sorry, I'm a schmuck, make that "the broad" – pushed a pen and a piece of paper (might have been an autograph book, I can't remember) towards Erimem. 'Could we have your autograph?'

She gave the regal smile. 'Of course.' She took the pen and inscribed a few characters before handing the book – yes, I remember now, it was an autograph book – back to da braod. 'Here.'

The woman just scowled at the ornate characters on the page. 'What's that?'

'My name,' Erimem replied patiently. 'In Egyptian.' She didn't actually sigh out loud but I know her well enough to know there was one in her head. She took the book back and used her English signature to the side of the hieroglyphs and cartouche she had done first. 'Wait. Now you have it in both languages.'

That certainly made the old broad happy. 'Thank you.'

'Are you doing another movie?' the husband asked.

'We have a sequel to the last film,' Erimem nodded.

'I'm so looking forward to that,' the old broad gushed.

'So am I,' Erimem agreed with the most radiant of smiles. It was her Queen smile, which I suppose just about fit in with being an actress.

The broad was ready to gabble some more until Helena interjected. 'Talking of the new movie, we have to get you to the studio,' she said, easing Erimem away from his little fan club.

'Oh, we totally understand,' the old broad said. 'We won't hold you up. We just love the movies.'

Erimem gave that superstar smile again. 'Thank you. I hope you enjoy the new film.'

'Oh, we will, we will,' the broad gushed.

She was still talking as we piled into cabs and drove away.

We didn't go to the studio as Helena had said we would. Instead, we drove to the house we had rented last time we were in 1940 Los Angeles. We knew we'd be coming back to we'd arranged a long term lease and retained a housekeeper, Rosa. Her welcome was a bit of a mixed bag, to be honest. A big smile and then volcanic fury.

'You're back! Why didn't you tell me you were coming? I didn't know. I don't have food or rooms ready!'

'Hello Rosa,' Erimem said in her most placating voice. 'We have missed you.'

'Rosa is our domestic manager,' Helena explained to Adam. Actually, she didn't. It was me, but it was such an obvious and dumb thing to say I didn't want to own up to it. Sorry, Helena.

Rosa didn't buy my description. 'I'm the housekeeper,' she said.

My answer was quick. 'You got promoted.' Okay it was also crap but it was quick and crap.

Rosa led us through into the main reception room. 'I wasn't sure you were coming back. I've been feeling guilty about drawing a salary.' She had been earning her pay though. The place was spotless.

'We'll be here when we need to be,' Helena explained. 'Other than that, we'll probably be away working elsewhere.'

That seemed good enough for Rosa and she started thinking about the practicalities. 'There are more of you this time. I'll prepare extra rooms.'

'Just one,' Helena said, 'for Tom.'

Tom raised a hand in greeting. 'Hi.'

Whoa! The temperature dropped about ten degrees and Rosa's eyebrows shot up to the roof. 'And the others?'

Erimem introduced Adam to Rosa. 'Adam is my... well, he is my...' She floundered over the word to describe him.

Helena again dug her out of a hole. 'You get the picture, Rosa?'

The housekeeper nodded. 'I do.' She looked at Tom briefly and then at Olivia. 'And this young lady?'

I fielded that one. 'Is *my...*'

Well, that was like somebody had thrown a bucket of cold water over Rosa. 'Oh... oh... oh, my...' I guessed there would be a couple of Rosaries said for us at the nearest church on Sunday. Looked like lesbians were still a bit of a shock to the system in 1940.

'And that's something we keep inside the house,' Helena said pointedly.

That didn't sit too well with Rosa but she Well, this is Hollywood, I suppose. I'm sure you're not the only ones.' She shrugged, gave us a smile and patted my arm. 'I'm not sure who I'd tell anyway.'

I had always got on well with Rosa. I can't tell you how relieved I was that she hadn't run screaming out of the place. 'Thanks, Rosa.' She gave me another smile. Yeah, we were going to be cool.

'So,' she asked, 'how long are you planning to be here?'

'That's a bit up in the air,' Helena answered.

Erimem agreed. 'We are not entirely certain yet.'

Rosa rubbed at her chi. 'Well, it will be a while. You have mail. A lot of mail.'

Well, Rosa wasn't kidding about the mail. There was the usual guff mail everybody gets. We got junk mail and spam mail even in 1940. Most of it was selling something. Rosa had dealt with the dull stuff – the bills and so on. The bulk of the mail, though, was fan mail. Erimem's first reaction was to laugh like it was a big joke. More than six and a half thousand bits of fan mail, forwarded by the studio. Six and a half thousand for some crummy little movie?

I got four.

If you are even thinking of laughing about that I will not be happy. I was not the star of the film, just the scene stealing minor performer. I should also say, two of mine were as close to pervy as you get for 1940.

So, dealing with my fan mail took all of two minutes, whereas we split Erimem's between us. The plan was for us to take a day sitting around in a group, reading the good ones aloud, deciding who got signed photos, and who should get a visit from da cops for being a bit suspect. And I'm going to stop saying "da" instead of "the". I can feel my IQ dropping every time I do it.

There was other movie mail, too. Erimem had some letters from the studio, most of which she should have answered ages ago. Although since she seemed to have answered them I guessed we would have to make some time in future to answer them in the past. The most recent was pretty clear, though. Preparations were under way for The Jewels of Cleopatra, the follow-up to Warrior Queen of the Nile and they wanted to talk to Erimem about it.

Adam read the letter over Erimem's shoulder. 'You're due at the studio tomorrow?'

She nodded. 'So it seems.'

We'd got lucky in turning up when we did. A day later and we'd have missed her appointment with the studio. 'We're going to have to find a way to forward the mail from here,' I said.

Erimem wasn't as concerned as me. 'I only make three films.'

'That we know of,' I argued. 'IMDB is not perfect.'

That knocked Adam sideways a bit. 'You have an IMDB page?' he asked Erimem.

I answered. I was on a roll by then. 'And I don't. There's no justice.' I mustered a wistful sigh. 'My knockers looked great in that last film. Okay, so the dress was engineered like something by Brunel but still... And as for my singing... you'd never believe how good I sounded.'

Nobody was buying the outrage. Guess I'm not that good an actress.

'We didn't,' Helena said. 'You were dubbed.'

I wafted a dismissive hand and went all Vivien Leigh. 'Hush now. Don't spoil the magic of the movies.'

Ah, it was good to be back in Hollywood. And this time there were no zombie Nazis.

STONE

Curtis Jennings was an ass. I'd call him worse but I been cleaning up my language since I got married. I been cleaning up a lot of things.

That should be "I've been". I've been cleaning up my grammar, too.

I married a wife who was too good for me, and too good to tell me she was too good for me. Or even think it. That meant I had to get my act together. No more wild boozing. No more wild dames. No more fights.

I married Lisa Borden after she saved my life. Okay, so she turned me into a zombie to do it but hey, nobody's perfect.

And I got better.

I got over being a zombie and I was normal again. As normal as I get.

Normal and a man desperate to prove to his wife that he might just deserve a knockout dame like her.

After we got married I took a job – a steady, paying, salaried job – as head of security at Centurion Pictures' studios. It was an easy number. We didn't have many big stars. Hell, we didn't have *any* big stars. Centurion made cheap and cheerful movies. Well, cheap, anyway. You know, that's not fair. Most of our pictures weren't bad. Movies were different back then. Movies were the only game in town except for radio. And the movies were a cheap night, too, so people went two or three times a week. There were lots of theatres in towns so there had to be plenty of movies to fill them. Sure, we didn't win any

Academy Awards but we put asses on seats.

And sometimes we put asses in director's chairs.

Yeah, Curtis Jennings was a real ass.

Jennings was a theatre director. He had a hit in New York with a play about... oh, who cares what. It was a hit anyway. He took it to Boston and then he brought it to LA. Centurion, for some unknown god-damned reason – sorry, I promised Lisa I'd stop cussing, I'll try again. Centurion, for some unknown reason, picked up the play and Jennings took their low-ball offer because they let him direct the movie. He did a decent job and the film made a lot of cash. For the studio, not for Jennings. Like a lot of smart guys, Curtis Jennings was dumb. As a rock. He signed his contract without reading the fine print first. Hell, even I read mine first. More important, my wife read it and told me to get changes made to it, which I did. The studio boss liked me. I'd helped him out a few times but we don't need to talk about that.

But it was dames.

With bosses it's nearly always dames.

Jennings thought he had signed a contract to make that one movie, whatever the hell it was about. Yeah, nobody gets a one picture deal in Hollywood, ya putz. He signed a seven year contract at Centurion and that meant he had to direct whatever picture they gave him. He didn't like it. He wanted to be released from his contract so he could do some Dickens adaptation. He even tried to get the boss to do Dickens at Centurion. No, that wasn't going to happen. You ever read Dickens? I mean, read all the way through one of his books. Me neither. I tried. Lisa bought me gorgeous hardback copies of a couple and I pretended to read them for her sake but I guess I just prefer an easy story of a guy who can punch his way out of trouble. "It is a far nobler thing I do right now to sock you in the mouth, pally."

Remember I said Jennings was dumb? Well, he proved it. He thought he could buy his way out of his contract. Now, that is not an unusual thing. Well, it's not common but it has happened in the movie business, right? Sitting on his cloud of ego, floating along on his one hit movie, Jennings offered the boss twenty big ones, twenty grand, to let him out of his contract. He'd heard that Jack Warner wanted to corner the classy end of the market. My boss was a savvy guy. He would not turn down twenty grand for anything, especially if it got a dumb-ass director out of his hair, not that he had any hair, but you get my drift. So it was a deal. Twenty grand and Curtis Jennings was out of his contract and didn't have to direct *The Jewels of Cleopatra*. I was kinda glad he wouldn't be involved. Me and Lisa, we were pretty friendly with Erimem and her buddies. She was the star of the picture. Turns out she was also some kind of British secret service agent. They all were. If you think dames got no place being agents and they can't fight, you should see these gals in action. Fists and feet flying everywhere. I never saw anything like them before. They're loyal too. They stood by me when most people would have run. They helped Lisa save me. I owed them. And more than anything, they're our friends.

I keep saying Jennings was dumb but so far I haven't said why he's dumb. Well, apart from trying to make a move on Lisa – she dealt with that by just pointing at me and mentioning that I carry a gun – he made a deal with the boss for twenty grand when he was lucky to have twenty bucks to his name.

That's when he acted dumb.

Everybody in LA had heard of Boss Peterman. He was a Swede and had some unpronounceable Scandinavian Christian name so he went by the name "Boss". And he was a big boss in LA. Clubs, brothels, extortion, protection, he did the lot. But he had a weakness. Everybody has one and his was the movies. He saw Jennings as his way into the flicks and Jennings saw him as his way out of Centurion, so he borrowed the twenty grand from Peterman through Peterman's lieutenant, Pat Daly. Jennings should have been smarter. Pat Daly was a bastard. He'd thank me for saying it, too. He put the hurt on people for fun and if he really needed cheered up, he killed the poor sons-of-bitches. It was always said that when Pat died and went to Hell, they wouldn't let him in because he scared them too much.

Jennings had his twenty grand but my boss didn't like to be played by anybody so he took a fortnight to go to New York to see some plays and scout some new actors. And then he stayed away because he was a mean old cuss. He was back in LA but everybody thought he was in Europe. Nobody at other studios would talk to Jennings because he was under contract to us. That meant that Jennings' plan to talk Jack Warner into hiring him for the Dickens movie – and get a twenty grand advance on his fee – wasn't happening. If I read Jack Warner right, there was no way he would pony up twenty big ones to Jennings anyway. Pat Daly wanted to talk to Jennings, though. In the month since the loan was handed over, that twenty grand debt had turned into twenty five. Another fortnight would turn it into thirty. That was when Jennings knew he was screwed. If nobody else could hire him, he couldn't get paid so he could pay off his debt. And if he couldn't pay off his debt...

And then Jennings got really stupid. With twenty grand in his pocket and a mob boss biting at his ass, Curtis Jennings decided to run.

I got the first inkling something was wrong when I got called to the front office. That usually meant there was something bad going down. But the first thing I saw when I opened the door was a heap of friendly faces. Erimem, Andy, Ibrahim and Helena all smiled, big and cheesy. I've been a miserable SOB most of my days. I only just got used to Lisa smiling every time she saw me, and I was pretty sure she only did it because she had to – some weird rule of marriage. God knows I always smile whenever I see her. But there were these four faces smiling at me and it was genuine warmth and friendship.

'Mr Stone,' Erimem said. I am a happily married man but she looked a million bucks in that white two piece and hat.

'Stone!' Andy was closest and she gave me a hug I sure wasn't expecting. 'How are you feeling? Completely over being a zombie?'

'Pretty much,' I answered. I gave Helena a grateful nod. 'Thanks again for that, doc.'

'All part of the service.'

Ibrahim shook me by the hand. 'Married life suits you.'

You know what? I think he was right.

Andy completed the introductions. 'These are our friends, Olivia, Tom and Adam.' A real pretty girl gave me a friendly smile. The guy introduced as Tom looked shifty and I got the idea he had something happening behind those eyes. He was harbouring some kind of hurt. The third of the newcomers, Adam, was a cop. I used to be a cop myself. We can spot each other a mile off and this Adam had it written all over him.

'I didn't know you were coming back,' I said.

Helena nodded towards Erimem. 'Miss Superstar has a new movie to make next week.'

I knew she was supposed to come back but I just hadn't been sure. They were agents, their country was at war... I hadn't been sure. But I played along, in case anybody in the room didn't know these guys had a double life. 'The Jewels of Cleopatra?' A circle of nods answered me. 'I should have known. Lisa's working on that one.'

That pleased Erimem. 'Is she well?' she asked. 'Is she happy?'

'I think I'd say "yeah" to both of those,' I answered. 'She'd be pretty pis...' I bit off the cuss. 'She'd be disappointed if you didn't ask her for yourself.'

'I will do so,' Erimem answered. If a sentence could sound like a salute, that was it. Yeah, there was no way I could forget she was a soldier.

'Sorry to interrupt,' Milt said. He was the producer of the movie and the one who had sent for me. I felt sorry for his mom. The guy had to have been born with a broom handle up his ass. 'Much as a love tear-jerker reunion, that ain't why I sent for you, Stone.'

That didn't sound good. 'No? Why am I here then?' Always best to get straight to the point with jackasses like Milt.

'We lost our director,' Milt told me.

'He's dead?' Did I sound hopeful when I asked that?

'No.'

'Joined the opposition?'

Milt was looking ticked off. 'No. We just can't find the bum.'

'So?' I shrugged. 'Maybe he took off with a broad. Or maybe he took off with a guy.'

'Don't be crude. There's ladies present.' Milt was a prissy little weed.

'Don't mind us,' Andy said pleasantly. 'We really don't mind. You have *no idea* how much we don't mind.'

'I don't care what side he butters his toast,' I told Milt. 'Maybe he's taken a day off. Maybe he's sick.'

'If I had the Peterman mob chasing me I'd be sick too.' Shit. Milt had just hit me with four aces.

'Peterman?'

Milt nodded. 'Seems our director borrowed some money from Mr Peterman and now isn't taking their calls.'

That changed everything. It was pretty much the dumbest bunch of choices I'd come across in a long time. And I've met Nazi zombies. 'Okay,' I said. 'What do you want me to do?'

'Find him,' Milt said. 'Bring him back here. If he don't want to come, slap him a few times and bring him back here.'

'And if Peterman's guys get to him first?'

'We'll send flowers to the funeral,' Milt said.

Erimem had been taking this all in. The whole gang of them had been listening. 'This man is in danger?' Erimem asked.

'Big trouble,' I answered. 'He borrowed big-time from a local hood.'

She smiled and looked excited. 'I know what that means,' she said to Andy. 'You showed me *The Godfather*. I understand that reference.'

'Proud of you for remembering, love,' Andy said, 'but maybe not the time to be excited?'

Erimem instantly turned serious again. She changed on a dime. 'You are right. If he is in trouble, he needs help. Mr Stone, I will come with you.'

'Like hell,' Milt yelped. 'You got costume fittings, make-up tests, we need to meet your stuntman...'

'Stunt*man*?' Andy said slowly. 'You think you can get a man to look like her?

Milt shrugged. 'Hey, I know there are stuntwomen but we don't have any.'

'Why?' Andy demanded. 'They've been around for twenty five years.' She glanced at Helena. 'Got to love a module on sexual equality in Media Studies.'

Milt tried to dismiss her. 'Yeah, whatever you're talking about, we don't have none.'

'You do not need one,' Erimem said calmly. 'I did my own stunts last time and I will do them again this time.'

'Like hell,' Milt snorted again. 'Last time you were a nobody. It didn't matter if you got killed when a stunt went south.'

'It would have mattered to her,' Andy said sourly.

Milt ignored the interruption. Dumb move, man. 'Toots here is the star of this picture. We can't have her getting hurt.'

Andy winced. 'If you call her "Toots" again, she's not the one who has to worry about getting hurt.'

Milt snorted that way he did. You may have worked something out about Milt. He was dumb as a rock when it came to people. I decided to cut him some slack.

'Erimem was a soldier back home,' I told Milt. 'Damn good one from the last time I saw her fight.'

'You've seen her fight?' Milt was starting to get the idea that he all wrong on this.

'Yep,' I answered. 'How many Nazis was it you took down in that old house, Erimem?'

'Four,' she answered.

'And then there were the punks in the alley. I heard about that.' I sighed. 'I wish I'd seen it.'

Ibrahim had cottoned on to what I was doing. 'It was impressive,' he admitted. 'Did you know they were armed with knives and she wasn't?'

'Not quite true,' Helena countered. 'She did have a bin lid. Make that a *trash can* lid. And there were only five of them.'

'Only five?' I thought Milt was getting scared. I should have known better. 'We could save a few bucks if we didn't need one of the stunt guys,' he said eagerly.

Yeah, Milt's all heart.

'She can handle herself,' I assured the producer.

'But we need her here right now,' Milt protested. 'You can find somebody else to back you up. One of the gorillas you have on security.'

My guys were good in a fight but I got the feeling I'd need a brain as well as muscles. 'They're busy,' I lied. 'I'll go alone.'

'I'll go with you.' The guy who had been introduced as

Adam took a step towards me. Yeah, I was right. He was a cop. No doubt about it.

'If he's hurt you might need a doctor,' Helena said.

'And I'm buggered if I'm being left behind,' Andy said.

'You can't go,' Milt said to Andy. 'It's in your sister's contract that you have to be in all of her pictures so you need fitted as well.'

Andy's face fell. 'Arse biscuits.'

'I'll come too,' Ibrahim said. 'Can't let my wife have all the fun.' He turned to the youngest guy in the group. 'Tom?'

Christ, the kid looked terrified. He wasn't like the rest of them. They had a kind of confidence to them. A real assurance in themselves. This Tom kid didn't have it.

'Maybe Olivia would rather go?' Tom said. Damn he was one of ours, American. It was a pity that the only one who was timid was ours.

The girl he'd called Olivia shook her head. She was a pretty girl – and pretty attached to Andy unless I got things confused – shook her head. 'I'd rather stay here, please.'

That seemed to surprise everybody, but I wasn't going to judge. Maybe she just wanted to soak in being in a movie studio.

'Okay,' Tom said reluctantly. 'I'll go.'

I didn't think he'd be much good in a fight. Helena and Ibrahim knew how to defend themselves and I never met a cop who couldn't scrap his way out if he had to. This kid, on the other hand... 'It's not compulsory,' I told him. 'You'll see more pretty girls here in the studio. Stay if you want.'

He looked at me like I'd called him a coward and slapped him in the kisser. 'I'll come,' he said and made for the door.

'Okay,' I said.

I knew that wasn't going to end well.

ANDY

Okay, I was surprised that Olivia hadn't wanted to go with Helena and Stone and the rest. Let's face it, she's a criminal. Or was. She was – three hundred years ago – a pirate captain, so breaking the law is right up her street. She's good at it, too.

And yet she was staying behind to watch Erimem and me get fitted for our costumes. I'm pretty sure she wasn't just hanging about to have a perv at me walking about in my undercrackers – even though I do look fab in 1940s lingerie, by the way. It may be as uncomfortable as hell but I look a million dollars in it, even if I do say so myself. Mind you, everybody looks look in this stuff. It heaves and shoves everything into place until you do. I just hoped my boobs would go back to their normal shape after being turned into cones by a 1940s bra.

For somebody who wanted to stay behind, Olivia was pretty quiet. That started to worry me. Once Erimem got dragged away to try on what they called her "fighting tunic". Before the door had even closed I heard her say, 'I am *not* wearing *that*!' I believed her. I love her to bits but she's a stroppy moo when she wants to be.

Says the stroppiest moo in moo-land.

'You're quiet,' I said to Olivia. 'Something up?'

She looked startled, like I'd shouted at her. 'Am I?'

I gave her my "are you really trying that bullshit with he?" look. In a shock to everyone – especially me – it worked.

'I have been thinking,' she said.

'I wondered what the noise was. Must have been the gears in

your head.' My sparkling wit crashed and burned. No laughs. I tried something else. 'Okay, what are you thinking about?'

'Us,' she answered simply.

My stomach dropped and I had the horrible feeling that I was going to throw up. Well, shit. I was going to get dumped by my girlfriend, and I was going to get dumped in a back room at a crummy studio in 1940 Hollywood. The *where* didn't matter but I was already grabbing at reasons to be extra miserable.

My voice sounded dry. That's because my mouth had suddenly gone very dry. 'And what about us?'

'How long have we been seeing each other?' she asked. Christ, she was going to stretch it out.

'Hard to say,' I answered. 'With time travel it's complicated. But... a couple of years.'

She nodded. 'I'm not sure either. I should be more precise. I know how old I was when we met and I know how old I am supposed to be now.' She paused and I really didn't like that pause. It was the axe being raised. Better to get the execution done and over with.

'What's this about, Olivia?'

'It is about...' she swirled a hand around us. 'This. Us. You and I.' She dropped her voice. 'Us together.' She shook her head. 'There is a lot of uncertainty in our lives. I don't think I can carry on with that.'

And there it was. A clean swing of the axe and we were done. Shit.

Just... shit.

I knew she had been thinking about something for a while. She had been spending more time in our time. Well, *my* time. I thought... didn't matter what I thought, did it? I suppose that is what a kick in the bollocks feels like.

Fuck.

I had to do something or I would just get emotional and I didn't want that. If that was it, then that was it. I'd known it was too good to last. There had been a little something gnawing at me saying it wouldn't last. Proper happiness wasn't for me.

'Okay,' I said, 'if we're done, then we should probably finish things cleanly. I'll get you back to your ship and time and...'

'What are you talking about?' Olivia fairly squeaked that. 'I do not want to finish our...' she looked around before whispering 'relationship.'

Okay. Now I was as confused as buggery. 'Then what are you talking about, woman?'

She was as exasperated as I was and really uncomfortable about it as well. 'I don't want to go back to the ship either.'

All I could manage was a confused 'So...?'

'*Ever*,' she added. 'I don't want to go back to the ship *ever*.'

Right. Okay. Listen, I'm supposed to be quite clever. If you ever hear that again, ignore it. I am clearly a stupid mare. I have been a stroppy moo, a dozy mare and at breakfast I made a pig of myself. I am a one woman farmyard. And I am a muppet. I finally got what Olivia was meaning.

'You want to move to 2020?'

She nodded vigorously. 'I don't want to wonder if it will be months before I see you.' She grabbed at my hand and whispered, 'I want to be with you.'

Suddenly it wasn't such a shit day. Suddenly, I've got my girlfriend asking... what? Was she asking to move in? That's a big step. *Really big*. On the other hand, saying no would be a stupid thing to do.

'Are you saying you want us to move in together?' Best thing is to be up front. Besides, I couldn't think of any other question.

Another nod. 'Yes. I think so.'

Right. That would need some thought. I was out and happy with that but living full time with another person. That had been hard enough when it was my brother – though in fairness he was and still is a twat. Okay, I had to put her off, stall, play for time to give this some thought.

'Okay,' I said. 'When can you move in?'

Betrayed by my own mouth. What a traitor!

And then Olivia's mouth was on mine and, yeah, right decision.

I heard the door open and then slam shut quickly. Outside, Erimem's voice said loudly. 'And I am *still* not wearing that... thing!'

Two seconds later she pushed the door opened and entered serenely with a startled looking woman from the costume department. Olivia and I had used those seconds to jump apart a few feet. Erimem had obviously seen us and bought us some time by playing the diva. I mouthed a quick "Thank you" at her. She smiled back with a slightly puzzled look on her face.

And then the costume department woman started talking and everything had to be put aside for a while.

I was surprised at the way I'd come close to falling apart when I though Olivia was dumping me. I thought I had hardened up over the past few years. That's when it really started to sink in. She wasn't just a girlfriend. She was fun, she was goofy, she had some bizarre old notions because she's learning about a world three hundred years after her own, but she was trying. She was a hundred things I can't put into words, but the big one was, she was the face I wanted to wake up with every day. And she wanted to be with me. That made me pretty happy.

On his way out, Stone had mentioned to Lisa that we were here. She looked in around then and there were more hugs and hellos.

Marriage suited Lisa Stone. She had always had a confidence I liked. She was relaxed with it now. She was running the set decoration department as well. Running it well, too. She acted as a peacemaker between Erimem and the costume woman and they came to a compromise. I'd have thought the director should have been involved in that, but if he was on the lam from the goodfellas then nobody wanted to hear his yap.

And that really doesn't sound at all right in an English accent.

STONE

The place to start looking for Jennings was at his apartment. He lived on the edge of a nice part of town. Kind of a frayed and shabby edge. It was a place you'd live if you wanted to look good on paper. The facts... yeah, they weren't so great. The building looked run down and in need of care and the building supervisor looked like he had just been run down. He had a lifeless look about him. I don't mean like a zombie – trust me, I've had my fill of zombies – no, this guy was worse. He just had a dead look in his eyes. It was like life was just too much trouble so he had decided to die inside and wait for his body to catch up.

'More than my job's worth.' That was the answer he gave when I told him I needed to get into Jennings' apartment.

'Is explaining why you have to fix the door after I kick it in likely to be a fun part of the job?' I answered.

That made him squirm. 'You kick any doors and I'll call the cops.'

'If you want the police I'm already here,' Erimem's guy said. He was quick, sharp and he put real attitude in what he said. Yeah. Something told me this guy was a good cop.

'You're a cop?' the supervisor asked.

'That's what I just said, isn't it, numb-nuts?' Adam answered. He nudged me. 'And this is a detective, so open the door before we do.'

I think his accent helped. There's a real hard edge in that Scottish sound. The supervisor shrunk. Damn, could I copy that accent?

'Well, if you're cops I suppose it's okay.'

The super led us up to the second storey. Jennings' apartment was at the end of a hallway. The super opened the door but I put an arm in from of him to stop him going in.

'We'll take it from here.'

Adam pointed at the nearest door on the hallway, maybe five or six yards back. 'Stand there,' he told that super. 'Make sure nobody comes closer than that. Understood?'

The super nodded. We left him out there in the hallway and closed the door behind us.

Just inside the door, Helena caught the American kid's arm. 'Tom, would you stay here, please. Listen for our friend out there in case he creeps closer. Let us know if he does. It's important. We need to be able to talk freely without him earwigging.'

The kid nodded. 'Okay.' He looked relieved to be useful.

I've got to say, Jennings may have been an ass but he sure kept a neat and tidy house. Everything was in its place, nothing looked like it was anywhere except where it belonged. That told me one thing. I'll be honest. It told all of us something.

It was Helena who said it. 'Nobody's been here before us. Everything is too tidy.'

Jennings loved books. He had shelves of them. All of them big and solid and probably as boring as hell. Sorry, I'm just not a reader. Even with the paper I start at the sports pages before I hit the funnies and if I have to, the news pages. Okay, that's not quite true. I like to know what's happening in the world, especially with that A-hole Hitler and his bunch of goons causing havoc over in Europe. Last time Erimem and her buddies were here, we had trouble with Nazis. I really hoped this wouldn't be a repeat.

Ibrahim had stopped the books as well. 'Classics,' he said. 'Dickens, Hardy, Jane Austen, the Brontes...'

Helena was only half paying attention. She was leafing through mail that was on the mantel. 'I liked Jane Austen. Did I tell you I have a first edition of "Pride and Prejudice"? She autographed it for me.' She flipped through a few more letters. 'Nothing interesting here.'

'There's something missing here, though.' That was Adam's voice from the bedroom. We went through and found him looking into clothes drawers. The neat assembly was disturbed and uneven. 'Clothes have been taken out in a hurry,' he said and then pointed at an empty space on top of the wardrobe beside a small suitcase. 'I'd bet money there used to be a bigger suitcase up there.'

Helena brought a sturdy wooden chair across and hopped up onto it. How the hell can women move like that in heels? She only gave the top of the wardrobe the briefest look. 'And the hunky Scotsman wins five pounds. The dust says there was something suitcase sized here.' She accepted Ibrahim's hand and dropped lightly to the floor.

'So he's done a runner,' Adam said.

'And you called him *hunky*,' Ibrahim added, bobbing his head at Adam.

'Yes, I did,' Helena smiled at Ibrahim. She was playing with him and they both knew it.

Ibrahim sniffed and glanced at Adam. 'You're not *that* hunky.'

'Yes, I am.' Adam was new since the last time I saw this bunch but he understood the way they worked. He got the rhythm of their conversations. The kid, Tom, didn't. Maybe he was the newest recruit.

Helena let Ibrahim off the hook. 'But he's Erimem's hunky Scotsman and you're my... well, you're mine.'

They should have been in front of a camera. They zinged together.

But I was there to work, not to enjoy these two sparking. 'So, he's definitely on the run.'

'Looks that way,' Adam nodded. 'Any idea where he would go? How he would get out of town?'

'There are plenty of ways out of this town,' I told him. 'Plane, train, boat, road.'

'Which one would you take?' Helena asked.

'Plane,' I answered.

'Why?'

'No way I'd take a boat. It's enclosed and it would be easy to get to the destination before the boat arrives.' I started warming to this, like one of those lawyers in our movies, setting out his case. 'The train and the bus have the same problem. Slow, you're stuck on board and you could have a nasty surprise waiting at the other end.' I thought for a moment. 'A car is a possibility, but unless he has a place to lie low he won't make the distance if he drives.'

'Which leaves the plane,' Helena nodded. 'Makes sense.'

'But that's you,' Adam said. 'Do you think he's got the sense to make the same decision you did?'

'Not a chance in hell.' The answer came out without thinking. 'He won't take the bus because he won't sit with the common schlubs. He won't take the boat because there's no comfort unless he splashes some cash and that will get him noticed. He's not driving. That doesn't fit his personality. He'll think the airports will be watched because they're obvious and fast. He'll travel on the train under an assumed name in a bad disguise.'

'Pretty much what I thought,' Adam agreed. There was no game there. Just one pro agreeing with another. Yeah. He was a good cop, all right.

'So the question is which station?' Ibrahim asked.

'If memory serves that depends on where he's going,' Helena said. She gave a kind of embarrassed smile. 'It's been a while since I used the trains here.' She tilted her head in thought. 'Or is Union Station open yet?'

'Opened in '39,' I answered.

Helena looked so damn pleased with herself. 'I thought so. Surely that's where he'll be.'

I nodded. 'I'd say so.'

'I'm not so sure.' Adam had spoken softly and he held up a hand to stop us asking questions. 'Don't anybody look, but behind me is a gold framed picture with who I assume is Jennings and his parents. It's lying on its back rather than on show.'

Shit. He was right.

'He wouldn't leave that behind,' I rumbled as soft as I can manage.

Helena saw what we were getting at. 'But it might be the last thing he'd pack. Something he would want to keep close.'

'Meaning he didn't finish packing,' I finished for her.

'No scuffle, no mess, so he wasn't taken forcibly,' Adam said. 'And the door was locked.'

His eyes flicked around the room. The inference was obvious. The rabbit was still in the warren, hiding somewhere. It wasn't a big apartment. It wouldn't take us long to find him.

The kid, Tom, came running. 'There's a noise out in the corridor. Men. I think they're giving the supervisor a beating.'

That had to be Peterman's goons. 'You packing?' I asked Adam. He shook his head. I retrieved the .38 from my ankle holster and tossed it to him then pulled my .45 from the shoulder holster.

The kid was right. There were boots stomping outside and a whine that sounded like the supervisor. Somebody had put the hurt on him.

Helena had disappeared for a moment. I hadn't noticed. When she came back she had three carving knives of various sizes she'd grabbed from the kitchen. She passed the longest to Ibrahim and held the other two, one in each hand, one pointed outwards and one pointed in, parallel to her arm in the style I'd seen some heavies from overseas use.

'Get behind us and stay back,' she told Tom. 'And if things get bad, get out of here. Got it?'

Tom nodded. The kid wasn't dumb. I kind wished she'd offered me the chance to haul my ass out of there.

Who am I kidding? No I didn't. I'd told Lisa I would live a quiet life, a peaceful life. I had been honest with her. Hadn't got into a fight since we got married. I hadn't been so drunk I woke up in yesterday's suit and somebody else's puke.

I'd lived that quiet life.

But I missed this buzz.

The door crashed in and four hired goons tumbled in. I spoke before they could react to us being there.

'That's far enough, boys.'

One of the gorillas reached for a pocket. It sagged under the weight of his pistol.

'Don't,' Adam said. The hand holding the .38 twitched just enough to stop the hoods from pulling their guns.

'So, boys,' I said, 'what brings you to a nice place like this? I didn't think they'd have 'roaches in this building.'

'That ain't nice, Stone.'

I knew that voice. Johnny Maldini. He was one of Peterman's

money men. We'd run into each other a few times. He'd tried to bribe me a few times when I was a cop. I'd told my sergeant about it. The sergeant had taken the bribe himself and told me to keep my mouth shut. Jennings was in trouble if Maldini had come looking for him personally.

'Well, I was never one for manners, Johnny.'

Maldini came in from the doorway. I got even more nervous when I saw Louise Spironi at his shoulder. Louie was a dumb son of a bitch but he was mean. He liked violence and he was good at it. Yeah, Maldini had come here to make Jennings hurt and hurt bad.

The hood was standing in front of his men. They looked more comfortable with Maldini there. It helped when there was somebody else there to think for them.

'I thought you were out of the game, Stone,' Maldini said.

'I am,' I answered. 'I'm just trying to find one of the guys from the studio. He hasn't been in for a couple of days.'

'You often check up on guys with a gang and guns at your back?' He glanced at Helena. 'Make that guns and knives?'

'When he didn't turn up we came to check,' I repeated. 'The lady's a doctor.'

'And she looks ready for surgery with those blades.'

I had to put that puck in the net. 'So don't give her an excuse to start.'

Maldini gave a fake smile instead. 'I won't.' He turned his attention back to me. 'So how about you tell me why you're really here?'

'I don't like the inference that I'm lying.'

'I don't like that you're lying, Stone.'

'Mr Jennings works for the studio,' I said. Maldini wasn't clever but he was cunning, always looking for an angle and expecting everybody else to be playing one, too. 'He offered the boss a deal and now he's on the run.'

'He ain't here?'

'Do you see him?' I snapped back.

Adam spoke. 'His suitcase is gone from the top of the wardrobe, his clothes are gone as well.'

'So you didn't find him?' Maldini was a suspicious bastard.

'Would we still be here if we had?'

Maldini looked around the place quickly. He noticed the bits of Jennings' stuff we had picked up and drew his conclusions. 'Trying to work out where he's going, huh?'

I played it cool. 'Maybe.'

That was enough of a confession for Maldini. 'And?'

'And nothing,' I said. 'Looks like he's in the breeze.'

You notice how I said that? *Looks like*. I didn't lie. It did look like Jennings was already on the run... if you didn't know what we knew.

Louie Spironi had to speak. He'd been getting jumpy. He knew why he was there and he wanted to show he was worth his pay check. 'I'll make them talk.'

I cut him down fast. 'You make a move, Louis, and I'll make you bleed, then I'll make you pray, then I'll make you squeal like a little girl.' My .45 was aimed straight between his legs. He got the message. He wouldn't be much use to that hooker he buddied with if I shot him there. She might thank me though.

'Easy, Louie,' Maldini said. Yeah, he was weighing up how much I was keeping from him. He wouldn't start a fight. He knew I'd shoot him first and I'd shoot to kill. 'Where do you think he's gone?' Maldini asked.

'I don't know,' I said. 'There's no receipts, no stubs, no letters from anywhere. We don't know where the little prick is.'

I dangled that insult against Jennings out there to see if Maldini bit.

He bit all right. 'Little prick? That's no way to talk about a colleague.'

'Colleagues turn up at work,' I answered.

You could actually see his brain working. It would have been funny if he wasn't a stone-dead killer. 'So he's got problems at the studio, huh?' Maldini asked.

I shrugged. 'If he's sick as a dog we brought a doctor to fix him. If he's cutting out on a deal?' Another shrug, lifting the .45 in my hand.

'What's the deal he has with your boss?'

'That would be somewhere between "what's it to you?" and "none of your damn business", Johnny.'

'Don't get smart, Stone.'

'Too late. I was born that way.'

Helena interrupted. 'If you two are quite finished with your dick-swinging contest...' Damn, there's something sexy when a polite-talking woman says something filthy like that.

'That ain't no way for a lady to speak,' Maldini said. I could tell he liked it too.

'I'll talk however I please,' Helena said. 'We're all looking for Jennings and none of us have found him here. Do you have any idea where he might be, Mr... Johnny, is it?'

'Johnny Maldini, and no, I don't know where he is or I'd be there picking him up.'

I knew what Helena was doing. She was smart. She'd picked up on me hinting Jennings wasn't there and pushed it.

'Are your people watching the airports?' she asked.

Maldini sounded insulted by the question. 'Naturally. That's the way I guess he'll try to leave, too. It's quickest. It's how I'd go.' He looked pleased with himself. 'But Mr Peterman's got eyes at the train station, the ports, on the buses. Whatever way this dumb mook goes, we'll catch him.'

'If you do, tell him the boss wants a word,' I said.

'Yeah. We'll do that.' The sarcasm dripped from him. 'You don't object if my boys take a look around?'

I shrugged again. Shrugs are big in gang communication. 'I won't stop you.'

A half laugh in reply. 'I know you won't.'

Maldini only came a few steps closer and gave a half-assed look around the room. He glanced into the bedroom, at the empty space on top of the wardrobe and the open drawer with clothes missing.

Shit.

The picture.

Maldini wasn't a brain surgeon but he wasn't dumb. That photograph might spark something in him. He didn't say anything about it. He came back and gave the room another look like it left a smell under his nose. 'Too neat,' he said eventually. 'A real man don't live alone in a place this neat.'

'You got a lady who comes in?' I asked. 'If you can call a broad who'd go to your place a lady.'

The insult didn't bother him. 'I hear you got a lady now, Stone. And word is she keeps Stone's stones in her purse.'

I didn't like Maldini talking about Lisa. I didn't like him *knowing* about her but I couldn't show that. 'I still get to use them sometimes.'

'There was a time you would have slugged me in the mouth for a crack like that, Stone.'

'Maybe I still will. Just not when you got your apes with you.'

Yeah, that got his attention. It was meant to. He stopped a half step too close and stared into me. 'That's more like it, Stone. The real you is still in there.'

'Let's both hope he stays "in there", huh?' I bit back.

Yeah, that was a threat. Maldini knew it.

He turned and walked away towards the door. 'Out, boys. There's nothing here for us here.'

Louie Spironi looked disappointed that he wouldn't be hurting anybody.

Maldini stopped at the door. 'Back off from this, Stone. This rabbit's ours. He ain't worth turning your wife into a widow over.'

'You talk about my wife again I'll put you in a box right now.'

Maldini just smiled. It's not a nice smile. Then he was gone.

I held up a hand to stop anybody talking. Helena looked at me like I was dumb as a rock. Yeah, like they were going to talk while Maldini's mutts could still hear us.

Ibrahim moved over to the door, looked outside then closed the door. 'They're gone. So is the supervisor.'

Adam was at the window. 'I see them outside. Two cars. There we are... wait, two of them are heading across to the alley opposite to watch the place.'

'That's hardly a surprise, really,' Helena said. 'Here and the studio are the two places they know he visited.'

That was what I thought. 'So they're watching here and the studio.'

'Wouldn't you?' Adam asked.

Helena decided to bring this to a head. 'That means you can't escape from the apartment, Mr Jennings,' she said in a louder voice. 'Eventually those thugs will come back and tear this place apart until they find where you're hiding. When they find you they will undoubtedly kill you, probably after some very painful and protracted torture.'

'Bet on it,' I agreed. 'Louie Spironi enjoys his work.'

'So,' Helena went on, 'you either trust the studio's head of security who is, despite what he said to those gullible idiots, here to keep you alive, or you hide like a mouse and wait to die. The choice is yours.'

Nothing. No answer. No sound, no movement. Just... nothing.

Helena didn't give up. 'Your choice, Jennings. Either you trust us or we just tell the two waiting downstairs that you're hiding up here somewhere.' She glanced at her wristwatch, a real fancy piece of work. 'I could say we'll give you five minutes to decide but I don't have the patience. Come out now or deal with Peterman's executioner.'

That was cold. I mean, really cold. I don't know if she meant it but she sure sounded like she did.

Jennings thought so too. A noise came from a little recess. Kind of an alcove. It was pulled back about two feet with shelves of books filling the top. An umbrella stand and some shoes made it look full and busy. The panel of wall starting at the level of the lowest shelf was being pulled back. Jennings' scared face looked out.

'All right. I'll give myself up to you if you promise you'll protect me.'

Helena looked at him for a moment. You could tell she didn't take to him at all. I always thought she was a good judge of character. 'Mr Jennings, you've already given up. You don't have a chip to bargain with.'

He swallowed hard. 'Are you saying you won't protect me?' He looked from her to every one of us, looking for some kind of comfort. He got slim pickings.

I cut the mug some slack. 'We'll do our best to keep you alive,' I said eventually. 'If we can get you out of here.'

'You have to get me out of this place. They'll kill me.'

He didn't get much sympathy from Adam. 'Maybe you should have thought of that before you ripped off their twenty grand.'

Jennings didn't have an answer to that. That was good. It

saved me sticking it back down his throat.

'All right,' I said. 'Is there a back entrance to this place?'

Jennings nodded enthusiastically. 'There's a door to the back. It leads to an alley that comes out round the corner.'

That was his way out. 'Be at the end of the alley in three minutes.'

Adam clamped a hand firmly on Jennings' shoulder. The little squirt winced at the pressure. Pretty sure that made Adam grip him tighter. 'I'll stay with him and sure he does.'

So that was how it worked. Four of us went down, got into the car, drove round a corner and Adam more or less threw Jennings in a second after I pulled up to the kerb.

'The arsehole wouldn't leave his suitcase,' Adam complained slamming the case on the car's floor. I pulled out into traffic.

'It's got my clothes in it,' Jennings protested. Jeez, I hated his voice.

'More likely it's got a gangster's twenty grand in it,' Ibrahim said.

Helena agreed. 'There's no other reason to cling to it like that.'

One look in the mirror showed what Helena meant. Jennings' knuckles were white in the handle of the case.

'You caused us a lot of trouble, you dumb ass,' I barked. 'What are you thinking trying to take Peterman's money?'

'It's *my* money!' His grip tightened on the suitcase handle as he squealed. Yeah. Helena was right. The dough was in the case.

'Where did you think you were going?' I asked.

'Away.'

Okay, so he was playing stupid. That needed to be slapped out of him damn fast. 'Listen, ass-hole, you keep giving us the smart-mouth and I'll drop you at Peterman's office then go home and have a nice dinner with my wife. The only thing you'll be eating is fists.'

'Careful, Stone,' Helena said. 'We don't want him to wet himself. It would ruin these shoes.'

'Talk,' Adam said. 'Talked before we get really pissed off.'

'I'm booked on a train,' Jennings said. 'Booked as Michael Cummings.'

I eased the wheel over and turned right. 'Well, that ain't happening. They're watching Grand Central and every other route out of the city.'

'So what am I going to do?'

'Hide him at the studio?' the kid, Tom, asked.

Helena beat me to the answer. 'They're watching the studio remember? We need to hide him somewhere else.'

I knew a few places that might be useful. But only might. 'There's a chance Peterman would be able to work out my usual bolt-holes. And no way in hell is he coming to my place.'

'Our place,' Helena said. 'Peterman doesn't know who we are, so he can't know where we live.'

Adam added to her suggestion. 'Plus we're surrounded by a high wall and means of access are limited.'

I'd never seen where they live. I mean, I'm security and they're... well, movie stars and spies. It ain't usual for me to mix with them. I've got to say, their place was pretty swanky. Big and bright with a pool and a neat garden, and I liked that high wall that ran around the place. The only real way in was through the front gates. They'd picked a pretty solid defensive spot. I'd taken the scenic route to make sure nobody had followed us. We left Jennings there with Ibrahim and the kid, Tom, then headed back towards the studio.

ANDY

Let's put it this way. Erimem was not happy. She threw the script for *The Jewels of Cleopatra* onto Milt's desk in disgust.

'I will not say these words.'

Milt looked surprised rather than scared. He just didn't know Erimem well enough yet. 'What's wrong with them?' he asked.

I answered. Less swearing if I beat Erimem to this one. 'Have you seen this script? It's rubbish.'

Milt snorted dismissively. 'It's a quickie. It was done in a hurry.'

'It was done in *crayon*,' I roared. 'It's garbage.'

Erimem wasn't shouting. Nope, she was more annoyed than that. 'I am not saying this. "By the savage fists of Ra?" It is shite.'

And there we have proof that having a Scottish boyfriend is rubbing off on her. "Shite" is so much more expressive than your bog-standard "shit". I raise my hat to her newfound cursing prowess.

Milt wasn't smart enough to be impressed. 'Listen, Toots. I don't need no broad giving me bellyache. Just do what you're told, like a good little girl.'

I didn't even need to look to know Erimem was moving towards him. I put an arm across her chest to stop her.

'Listen, friend,' I said quickly, 'I'm talking now, because if I don't stand between her and you, there will be nothing between you and a very lengthy visit to the dentist.'

'She wouldn't dare.'

Olivia had been standing to the side. She shook her head and turned away. 'Well, that was a stupid thing to say.'

She was right. Some people you just can't help. 'You're on your own,' I told Milt before turning to Erimem. Her eyes were burning holes into the producer. 'Should I call for an ambulance now or after?'

She moved a step closer to Milt and for the first time he realised that this wasn't the average studio-manufactured starlet who had been programmed to just do as she was told. He was a bit late to the party, but he started to look scared.

Erimem's hand shot out and he flinched.

He got lucky. She just scooped up the script. Her voice was ice cold. 'We will take this... *script* away and...'

I finished the sentence for her. 'Polish it, is, I believe the term.'

Having unexpectedly retained his teeth, Milt reacted like any money-man would. 'The sets are built, the cast is hired. You can't change any of that.'

'We will make it better,' Erimem said coldly.

She turned and fairly swept out of the room. Sometimes you really can see that she was Pharaoh of Egypt.

'She must like you,' I said to Milt.

He exhaled big-time. 'I'd hate to see how she is with somebody she doesn't like.'

'You're right,' Olivia said. 'You *really* don't ever want to see that.'

You know, I think that was what really scared Milt. Olivia had been the quietest of us. It was her first time in Hollywood. She wasn't gobby or bolshy the way I can be. She'd just told him the truth and it scared the crap out of him.

I gave Milt my cheesiest grin. 'We'll see you tomorrow. Have a nice night.'

And I hustled Olivia out before we pushed the weirdometer into overdrive.

Too late.

A minute later we were all back in Milt's office, only with Helena, Adam and Stone with us. I almost felt sorry for Milt. He thought he'd got rid of the troublemakers and we were back, doubled in size.

'We found Jennings,' Stone said.

Milt looked at the faces in the office. It wasn't a big office to things were a bit cramped and we were starting to squish together. We were certainly close enough for Olivia to squeeze my arse and have nobody notice. Honestly, you agree to move in with a girl and she thinks she can take liberties... I'm pleased to say...

Anyway, back on topic, Milt hadn't spotted Jennings. 'So where is the little putz? I don't see him.'

'That's because he's not here,' Stone answered.

'But Peterman's men are,' Helena put in.

Adam nodded. 'They're watching this place. Stone was right not to bring him here.'

'Was he?'

Stone glared at Milt. 'Yeah, I was, unless you want Peterman's boys paying us a visit to get their mitts on Jennings.'

Adam shrugged and turned the accent up a few notches. 'If they come, maybe you're the man to talk to them. Aye, you're a tough looking fella. Those guys with their guns and knives and razor blades, they'll respect you right enough.'

Okay, some present in the room didn't quite understand all of that but we got the gist.

Milt certainly did. 'I don't want to know where he is, but we need to find a way to sort this out. The boss doesn't want any mob boys around.'

'Then he shouldn't have agreed to accept a Godfather's twenty grand, should he?' That was Helena. Sometimes I think she failed her O Levels in subtlety and tact. Not that O Levels were invented when she was a kid. Hell, the UK or even England hadn't been invented when she was school age. Not that she could have gone to school back then. If you don't know her life story I'm not going into it. Just... she's older than she looks. I hope my boobs look that good when I'm over two thousand years old. But I'm off topic.

Milt was speaking. 'What's the plan?'

'Why are you asking me?' Stone answered. 'You asked me to find him and I did. That's my job done.'

'Not any more. Now your job is get a deal with Peterman that keeps us in the clean.'

'I thought your job was producer?'

Milt shrugged with his mouth. 'I can't produce with gangsters threatening the place. Find out what they want.'

'And if what they want is Jennings?'

Milt didn't want to answer that. 'Maybe you and me should talk in private, Stone.'

'And perhaps you should not,' Erimem said icily.

Adam agreed. 'Particularly if it involves selling Jennings to a gangster.'

'Nobody's selling Jennings,' Milt protested. 'We just don't want the studio involved in his deal with a hood.'

Nobody bought that.

'Bollocks,' Helena said. She has a way with words. Most of them filthy. 'Your boss agreed a deal with Jennings and is just trying to keep himself out of a villain's sights, and he'll sell that idiot out to do it.'

Milt didn't even blink at being called out for lying. 'Peterman is nobody's mug, and that hood of his, Louie Spironi? He enjoys hurting people.'

'He looked the type,' Helena answered. 'But there has to be a better answer than letting them use Jennings to try out a concrete overcoat.'

Milt gave the falsest of smiles. 'And that's what I want Stone to find.'

'We could just tell the thugs that you're Jennings,' I said to Milt. 'That way, when they drop you in the Pacific everybody's troubles are over.'

He wasn't sure if I was joking or not. Good.

'Just fix it,' was all he said.

Stone sighed. 'Damn.'.

STONE

After dumping this mess on me, Milt vamoosed from the office. He made like the big man, dropping hints that he was seeing one of the typing pool for a bit of recreation in the afternoon. It was baloney. Milt was too damn mean to share anything, and that included his bed. He just wasn't interested in women. He wasn't interested in men either. But any spark he'd ever had at the sight of an attractive face had upped and died. Hell, maybe it committed suicide because Milt depressed it so much.

There's a surprise that comes from having friends. They don't leave you to deal with problems alone. I was still getting used to having a wife who shared the bad times. Adam, Helena, Erimem, Andy... they all said they would help. I didn't know what I was going to do but at least I wouldn't be doing it alone.

'We have a dinner invite,' I told Lisa. I met her down in her workshop. She was working on trinkets for Erimem's movies. You know something? I would never have used a word like "trinkets" before I got married.

'Eating with the talent? What will that do to your tough guy image?' Lisa smiled. She was pleased and teasing me. I was pleased to be teased. I waited until we were driving home to tell her the whole story. The dinner was more than social. It was cover for me talking with Jennings. I felt like a heel because it took her smile away. She was game, though, and only let me see the disappointment for a second.

'Okay,' she said. 'What do we need to take?'

We dressed swanky. This was work but we had to put on the

show so we dressed like we were going to our glitzy buddies for dinner. Most of the time I look like a sack of potatoes in a suit. When I try to polish up, I look like a sack of potatoes in a good suit. Lisa? She always looks good. When she puts the glam on, she's a knockout. She could in the movies instead of behind the scenes. Okay, I know I'm biased, so sue me.

But I'm right.

We arrived at that damn big house of theirs and I was glad the gates closed behind us. If I was being tailed by Peterman's mugs I didn't want them any closer than the wall. They'd make the place look untidy and the gardener here had done a damn good job.

The door was answered by the same nice Mexican housekeeper who had been there earlier. She was giving Adam an ear of hurt for trying to answer the door. That's her job. He stood back and let the housekeeper, Rosa, see us in and take our coats. She let him off the hook and let him lead us into the main lounge. Damn, that really is one nice place. They got taste. Still, Erimem makes movies and they're on the British government's dime as a secret agent of some sort so I guess they're not short of a few bucks.

They were all sitting around, dressed up for dinner. I was glad we hadn't made the effort alone.

Lisa handed flowers to Erimem. 'I thought we should keep up the show. Besides we *are* your guests, even if it's not the average dinner party.'

'Thank you.' Erimem took the flowers. She looked surprised and kinda touched by the gesture. Yeah, that was all Lisa. The bottle of bourbon was from me.

'We've got some good Scottish stuff you can try, as well,' Adam said.

Damn, real Scotch. But I couldn't. 'Another time. I've got to drive later.'

Lisa let me off the hook. 'It's okay, hon. I'll drive home.'

'You sure?'

'I'm a better driver than you anyway.'

I accepted the drink from Adam. It had bite but it was smooth too.

'Glenmorangie,' Adam said. 'Forty years old.'

I raised my glass. 'Happy birthday to it.'

'Can I try it?' That was Jennings.

'No.' Adam, Ibrahim and I all said that at the same time. I'd refused because I didn't like him. I was surprised by the fire the other two gave their answers.

Jennings looked even more sheepish than usual. 'I already apologised for thinking he was a servant.'

Adam looked at Ibrahim and shook his head before turning to Jennings. 'And my friend isn't deaf.'

Ibrahim leaned forward and spoke quietly enough that none of the women heard us. 'Listen, you worthless little shit. You're not the first brain-donor to insult me because of my skin colour. You probably won't be the last, but if you do it again, I'll punch you in the face really hard, because while I don't care enough about what you think to be bothered, it really upsets my wife and anybody who upsets her right now gets their teeth to play with. Understood?'

Jennings nodded stiffly.

Adam smiled cheerfully. 'Incidentally, I'm a cop. A detective sergeant. And I'm not going to see what he does to you.'

Jennings had already paled. Now he went grey.

Good.

I know how some people get treated. The Mexicans get it bad here in LA. I don't like it. There's not a hell of a lot I can do about it but I don't have to like it and I don't have to let people get away with it when I'm around.

'Don't worry,' I told Jennings. 'Ibrahim isn't going to hurt you.'

Ibrahim looked surprised. 'I'm not.'

'Nope.' I shook my head. 'Because you're a professional. You might kill him. *I'll* hit him. I'll only break some bones.'

I should have been ashamed of what we were doing to Jennings but I wasn't. He had insulted my friend and he had stolen a heap of cash and caused this trouble. No, I didn't feel bad. Not one bit.

I was going to say we should sit down and talk over what we were going to do but Erimem beat me to it. We sat down and Rosa closed the door behind her as she left. We had about half an hour till dinner.

'How much money did you borrow from this gangster?' Erimem asked Jennings.

There was one stupid thing he could do at that point. He did it. 'Ten thousand dollars,' he lied.

Erimem spoke before anyone else could react. 'And how much do you still have?'

'Ten thousand,' Jennings answered. 'If I – or one of you – hand it back – will they leave me alone?'

That was when I decided never to play poker with Erimem. I couldn't read her at all. 'Do you think they would kill you if you handed it back yourself?'

'They're gangsters,' Jennings whined. 'If they see me again they'll kill me for fun.'

'Possibly,' Erimem bodded slowly. 'In fact I would say it is very likely.' She took a sip of her wine. 'Of course that would be because of the ten thousand dollars you still owed them.' She is not tall, but she has presence, you know? She can fill a room. 'We know you borrowed twenty thousand dollars from Peterman.'

Jennings looked around the room for support. He found cold faces and no sympathy.

'We all know,' Erimem added.

'So why did you ask?' Jesus he sounded like a kid.

'To find out if we could trust you,' Erimem replied.

'Epic fail on that front,' Andy said.

Helena was next. 'Lying to the people who are trying to help you? I'd call that the stupidest thing you could do, except you insulted my husband. *That* was the stupidest thing you could do. I'm sure he has spoken to you about it, but he is the nice one of us. I am a doctor and I know how to hurt you very badly. Don't ever insult him again.'

Jennings wasn't actually stupid, not in the way Louie Spironi is stupid, but Jennings wasn't smart. He had intelligence but he wasn't savvy. His smarts came from a book, not from life. He didn't know how to deal with people. He was going to talk his way into trouble here, so I saved him. I must be going soft.

'Just tell us the truth or we can't help,' I said. 'If you lie again, you're on your own with Peterman.'

Jennings nodded. I think that made me dislike him more.

'How much of the twenty thousand dollars do you still have?' Erimem asked.

'All of it.'

Well, that was something.

'I take it just handing the money back won't be enough?' Helena asked.

Erimem answered. 'The Peter-man has been insulted. A leader cannot take a slight like that without retribution. He must be appeased by a tribute of some sort. I do not know if he would prefer money or this man's head.'

'Does it matter which I prefer?' Jennings squeaked.

'No,' every one of us answered.

'We need to find out what Peter-man wants,' Erimem said. 'What he will find acceptable as a tribute.'

'He's a gangster,' Jennings shined.

'And you're a thief,' Andy said, 'so shut your cake-hole.'

It wasn't ladylike but it quieted Jennings. I like Andy.

'I guess it'll be my job to find out what Peterman wants,' I said.

'I'll come with you,' Adam offered.

I appreciated that. He'd handled himself well. When Ibrahim offered as well, that put some steel in my back. Ibrahim was quiet but he knew how to handle himself. The kid? Ibrahim suggested Tom stay here and keep an eye on Jennings. The kid looked relieved. He had looked like he would volunteer because he thought they expected him to.

So that was all decided pretty quick. I would phone and arrange a meeting to find out what Peterman would accept. The cover story would be that the boss didn't want bad publicity for the studio.

That was kind of the end of it. From there everybody got talking about the movie they were making, *The Jewels of Cleopatra*. Man, it sounded awful. Even Lisa thought it should have been flushed. We talked about it over dinner. Got to say, Rosa was a hell of a cook. The conversation was good, the friendship was real and the laughs were genuine.

They all had different relationships inside the group. Erimem and Adam were together. It was clear the way they looked at each other. Same went for Helena and Ibrahim. The same with Andy and the new girl Olivia. The difference was they tried not to show it. I guessed that was for us. We work in Hollywood. These are not the first girls who like girls we've seen.

Erimem and Andy are close as sisters should be. There's something family about the way she looks at Ibrahim. Helena? That's different. Affectionate and like they have a different bond. With Olivia she's warm and welcoming. Tom? She tried to include him but he was harder to draw into things. They all made an effort with him but he was hard work for them all. The rest? They had a rhythm in the way they talked and interacted. Have you seen the Marx Brothers? Each of the brothers has his own schtick, his own style. So do these people and they click together. I guess that make Tom the brother who didn't make it to the movies. Gummo, was it? I started to feel sorry for him.

But then the conversation caught me and I was laughing again.

Then Erimem started reading bits of her new script.

And we were laughing again at how bad it was.

ANDY

After dinner we went back into the big lounge and laughed a lot. We discussed the film script. We took it apart, threw the worst of it away, tried to come up with something better with the same characters and sets. The only film pro among us, Jennings, was worse than useless. He had zero-none-nada ideas. He was still wondering how he could escape with the twenty grand.

After an hour and a half we had laughed a lot but all we had come up with was rubbish scrawled by me on sheets of a notepad.

'This is still shit,' I said, tossing the pad to Erimem. I like to think I did it nonchalantly and with classic Hollywood style.

Lisa looked slightly startled at my potty-mouth. And then she relaxed. I think that was when she really felt she had joined the gang. 'It's not very good,' she agreed

Erimem caught the pad as stylishly as I threw it and she read the squiggles that passed for my handwriting. 'Yes, it is terrible. We are not writers.'

Helena sighed and gave a shrug. 'So you will just have to go with the script as it's written.'

Erimem wasn't having that. 'I would rather be dead in my tomb.'

'With jackals nibbling at your toes.' That sounded better in my head that when I said it out loud. That's three glasses of good wine for you.

'How would they nibble on my toes?' Erimem frowned. 'I would be inside my sarcophagus and the stone coffin. I would also be wrapped in bandages and...'

Yeah, she'd had some wine too.

'Off topic much?' I said. I tried to get us back to the subject. 'But you have to say something. The film gets made. We know it does.' Ooh, an idea was starting to waggle inside my head. 'We *know* it does.'

Thankfully the Stones didn't pick up on what I was getting at. I think they were making eyes at each other.

Helena had a thoughtful look on her face, though. 'I think you're on to something,' she said to me.

'Of course I am.' My smugness made a sprint for the door. My idea was still on the fuzzy side. 'Would you be a love and explain it to the room for those who have worked out my genius plan yet? People such as, oh, me.'

'The film *was* made,' Helena said. She whispered "was". 'It exists in our... Netflix collection. So?'

Finally I got it. So did Erimem. 'I understand. If I have already said it on film on Netflix...'

I finished for her. 'Somebody just has to nip back home and pick up a copy of the film so we can transcribe it.'

Helena waved a hand to cut me off. 'No need. You can get movie scripts online. Bet you it's on a site somewhere.'

I knew about script sites from Media Studies. I didn't fancy our chances, though. 'A cheesy little flick like this? Bet you a penny it's not.'

Fifteen minutes and a trip back to Erimem's Habitat to surf the internet brought me back to Hollywood weighed down with printed scripts and a laptop. 'Well, that's a penny I owe you all.'

Helena was more surprised than anybody. 'You found it?'

I handed the scripts out. 'And got it printed. Six copies, all looking like they were hand typed.' I bopped Erimem on the head with her copy before handing it over. 'That computer thing of yours is a thing of beauty.'

Ibrahim was peering over Helena's shoulder at her copy. 'What's the script like?'

I'd had a quick scan back at the Habitat. 'I think it's quite good,' I answered.

Helena agreed. 'This is clever dialogue.'

Adam was perched on the arm of Erimem's couch, reading

her script as she flicked through it. 'You're right. It is.' He shrugged. 'Though what do I know?'

Helena was the quickest reader. 'It's using the same characters and sets but it's a totally different story. A much better one.'

'Well done to the writer,' Ibrahim smiled.

'And that is who exactly?' Adam asked.

That was a good question. I didn't have a good answer – but I had a smart-arse one. 'It's not the blind monkey who scribbled that first thing we read.' I shrugged. 'But it's not us either.'

Ibrahim rubbed at his chin. He had taken to doing that. 'So who wrote it?'

I managed an 'Um...'

Erimem did no better. 'I...'

Adam leaned forward and spoke quietly, trying to avoid confusing the guests. 'That's a thing. *Nobody* actually wrote it, did they?'

Erimem frowned. 'Is that possible?'

Helena nodded slowly. 'Apparently so.'

I think I summed it up pretty well. 'Well, that's every kind of bat-shit crazy.'

'I think we are being rude,' Erimem said. She was looking at Stone and Lisa. They both looked kind of bemused. So did Jennings but we didn't care about him.

'Don't worry about us,' Lisa Stone said. 'We're fine.'

Stone took a deliberate sip of his whisky. 'Wondering what the hell you're talking about but fine.' He sounded suspicious.

'Just movie stuff,' Helena said. 'Nothing major.'

I gave Erimem my most sympathetic look. 'So, looks like you're back in front of the camera next week.'

'I think you should look at this,' Olivia said. She had the laptop. If she was looking at porn again...

We moved across to join her, ignoring Stone's questions about the laptop and what it was.

Nope, it wasn't porn Olivia was looking at; it was the film, *The Jewels of Cleopatra*. She had frozen the frame... frozen the frame with us *all* in it. Erimem, me, Helena, Olivia, Adam and Ibrahim. Even Stone was there in a big action fight scene. We were kicking the ever-loving shit out of some poor sods. Those stuntmen were earning their crust.

A broad smile spread across Erimem's face. 'It looks like we are *all* in front of the cameras next week.'

We kind of put the movie to bed after that. It just turned into a dinner party. We had been bad hosts so we made Stone and Lisa the centre of the rest of the night. She talked about the films she had worked on and what her ambitions were. Stone and Adam were talking cop stuff. Ibrahim was hanging with them. So was Tom, sort of, though he was on the edge of that conversation. By the time we realised it was late we realised it was really late. Lisa and Stone accepted the offer of a bed for the night to spare them a drive home at stupid o'clock. It meant we stayed up a bit longer. You know something? It was a weird night but a good night.

STONE

Okay, so we stayed over. Hey, who doesn't want to stay at a movie star's swanky house? Besides, it was fun. Jennings went to bed early. That made it more fun for the rest of us. I even warmed to the kid, Tom, a bit. Ibrahim explained that Tom felt guilty for his girlfriend's murder. That made me feel like a heel for being so down on him before. He's not easy to like but I can give him some slack for what he went through.

I always liked Ibrahim. He was the only guy in their gang before. He's not outnumbered anymore. I think him and Adam are buddies. They really get along. When we got to comparing cop scars – and every cop picks up scars along the way – Ibrahim had us both beat, showing where he'd been run through with a sword. He waited till Tom was out of the room to show that. I didn't expect that. I know these folks are some kind of British agents – I saw their ID passes first time we met – but I get the feeling there's even more to them than that.

It's a nice house. A *really* nice house. I knew Lisa liked it from the get-go. There was nothing wrong with our own place. She decorated it. She knew that stuff. So it looked great. It was comfortable. But this place had something else.

Even the bed was more comfortable.

They found new pajamas for me and a nightdress for Lisa that made this good dog want to go bad. Lisa had other ideas. She climbed into bed and snuggled close. She kissed me on the cheek and said, 'Don't even think about it. Not when we're guests in this house.'

Did I say how much I hate that house?

We fell asleep pretty quickly. It had been a long day, it was late and we were bushed.

A noise in the house woke us suddenly. My watch said ten after four. I thought it was Peterman's crew. I told Lisa to stay put and grabbed both of my pistols. The rest of the house had been wakened as well. They all spilled out of bedrooms in the weirdest pajamas and robes I ever saw. I was ready to toss Adam one of the guns when I saw him relax.

The ruckus was Erimem. She was dragging Jennings back into the hall by the hair. He was bleeding from the nose and the mouth and she was the one who had made him bleed. He looked terrified.

It was Andy who spoke. 'Okay, you were right. He tried to do a runner. I suppose that's a Coke I owe you.'

'She's crazy,' Jennings whined. 'She broke my nose.'

Erimem carried on up the stairs, still dragging Jennings by the hair. If she pulled any harder she'd scalp the schlub. 'He tried to punch me,' she said. She sounded offended that he had tried. I was more amazed that his head was still on his shoulders.

'She's a lunatic! She's crazy!' Jennings' foot slipped and he went down to a knee. She kept dragging his up the stairs.

'And you're pissing her off,' Andy said. 'By my reckoning that makes you the really crazy one.'

Erimem tossed a canvas bag to Andy. It clanked as she caught it.

'That doesn't sound like cash,' Helena said.

Andy opened the bag and pulled out a few bits of expensive looking silverware we'd seen about the place downstairs.

Jennings shrank.

'You stole our stuff?' Andy took a step closer to Jennings. 'You gobshite.'

He shrank some more.

'I should kick your bollocks in,' Andy told him.

Erimem snorted. 'I already tried that. I couldn't find them.'

I grabbed Jennings by the collar and pulled him upright. 'What were you thinking about?' I really I looked and sounded as disgusted as I felt.

He didn't answer. Didn't look us in the eye either.

'What do we do with him?' Ibrahim asked. He sounded like he was in favour of just throwing the guy to Peterman.

'I'll sit with him,' Adam said, 'just to make sure he doesn't try to run again.'

Erimem shook her head. 'No, everybody needs sleep. We should bind him.'

Adam was only wearing a pair of pajama trousers. He patted the pockets. 'I don't have my handcuffs. I left them at home.'

Andy started to speak. 'We've got...'

A lot of eyes turned to her. 'Yes?' Helena asked.

Andy shook her head and Olivia started to blush. 'Nothing,' Andy said flatly. 'Nothing to see here. Move along.'

That had the potential to turn real weird, real fast. I cut in. 'I have a set of cuffs, just in case I run into bad news. They're pretty useful knuckle dusters, too.' I didn't need to look to know Lisa was giving me *that* look. 'Just in case,' I added.

Erimem was all business and I was glad of it. 'Handcuff him to his bed,' she said.

'Okay,' I agreed. Adam came over to help me move Jennings.

Erimem finally let go of Jennings' hair. 'And if you bleed on the sheets, I will let Rosa deal with you.'

ANDY

The next morning we were back at the studio – well, some of us were – and we were in the producer Milt's office. He had a strange look on his face. It was like his face was trying to remember how to look happy.

'You rewrote this?' he asked. He was staring at the new script and then at Erimem and then at the script again.

'Well, not alone,' Erimem said evasively. 'We were all involved in making the decisions.'

Milt wasn't really paying attention to the answer. 'This is a great script,' he said, tapping his finger hard on the bound pages we'd given him. 'I mean, really great.'

Erimem nodded. 'I think so, too.'

She failed her O Level Modesty.

Milt's face reverted to a frown. I suppose it got scared by having tried to look happy. 'You know, you don't get paid extra for this.'

'Why does this not surprise me?' Erimem answered with acid dripping from every word.

Milt was flipping through the pages of the script, stopping at a scene for a reminder of a line then moving on. 'This dialogue is funny. It's peppy.'

This time it was Erimem who frowned. 'Is that a real word?'

'Peppy,' Milt exclaimed. 'It's got pep.'

'Is that a real word?' Erimem asked again, only more slowly this time, in case we hadn't heard.

'In 1940 it is,' I reassured her.

We didn't really need to be there. Milt was having a conversation with himself. 'We still need a director,' he muttered. 'It won't be Jennings. Who's available?' He started rummaging through papers on that fire-trap of a desk. 'We got nobody free… is there anybody we can borrow from another studio? Mike Curtiz is busy, so is Wyler. I wonder if Rouben Mamoulian…'

Erimem interrupted him. She had the imperious queen face on. 'We have a director,' she said.

Milt's eyebrows rose. His hairline was making a bolt for the back of his head so they had a fair bit of moving room and they made the most of it. 'Who?'

'Lisa Stone,' she answered.

Milt stared back, shocked. 'The dame from set decoration?'

He'd forgotten who else was in the room. 'My wife?' Stone rumbled.

Milt waved his hands to defuse tension with Stone. 'Hey. I'm just saying. Dames don't…'

That was what I'd been waiting for. I was in there like a Rottweiler. This was stuff I knew about old Hollywood. 'Dames do. There are women directing movies. Alice Guy-Blanche, Lois Weber, Dorothy Arzner.'

'Not for us,' Milt snapped. 'We don't have dame directors.'

'You do now,' Erimem shot back, in full Pharaoh mode. 'It is not a discussion.'

Milt looked set to argue but either he realised he was outnumbered or he accepted that Lisa was the only choice actually available to him. He conceded. 'If she falls apart it's on you.'

And that was the end of the discussion.

We left Milt's office and Stone stopped us in the corridor. 'Hey, I appreciate you doing this but shouldn't you ask Lisa first?'

I thought I knew why Erimem had made the call. Lisa had, quite shyly, said she'd like to direct, but them she'd laughed at the idea because… well, Centurion Pictures weren't the only studio with no women directing films. Female directors were still very rare. Hell, they're still something you notice in credits in movies in 2020.

Erimem shook her head and answered Stone. 'No. It must happen so it will.'

Yeah, that didn't mean anything to him. 'What made you think of Lisa as director?' he asked.

Erimem winked at me. 'I watched through the credits.'

Yeah, that meant nothing to Stone either. We'd made sure that he and Lisa never really saw any of the film the previous night.

It meant something to me, though. It meant I was really dumb. 'Oh. maybe we should have done that.'

'Maybe,' Erimem grinned sweetly.

Sarky mare. 'It's not like it's a Marvel film with extra scenes in the titles,' I protested. Her eyebrow lifted just a fraction. My shoulders slumped. 'What? It's got extra scenes in the credits?'

'One after them,' she nodded.

That was unexpected. 'Are we inventing the Marvel Universe here?'

She thought for a moment. 'It is possible that we are influencing it – but only after being influenced by it ourselves.'

I joined in the nodding. It seemed like the thing to do. 'They homaged us after we ripped them off? Cool!'

Stone was still none the wiser, and looking kinda grouchy about it. 'What are you talking about?'

'Don't worry about it,' I said. 'It's no biggie.'

Erimem gave her friemdliest smile. It defused most things. 'We like it when people don't know what we're talking about.'

Milt's door opened and he came halfway out of his door. 'You still here?'

'No, I answered sourly.'

Milt snorted. 'Wise ass.' He looked to Stone. 'What about you? You got work to do.'

Stone yawned lazily. 'We're going to meet Peterman's guy at ten to find out what they'll accept.'

Milt looked more interested. 'Where you meeting Maldini?'

'Fat Barney's place.'

Milt nodded. 'I guess nobody causes trouble there.'

'Not if they got sense,' Stone agreed.

STONE

You'd think it was kind of mean to call a guy Fat Barney. It never did Fatty Arbuckle any harm. Other bits of Arbuckle's reputation did that. But the name? Not so much. The thing about Fat Barney is that the guy is as thin as a rake and as straight as the crease on my pants when they come back from the cleaner. Every boss in the city has tried to get leverage on Fat Barney and nobody ever got their hooks into him. He just played fair with everybody, never let anybody get whacked or ambushed in his place and always stayed on the right side of the law.

Normally when somebody in my line – or the private eye line I used to be in – went into his place, Barney let them know he wouldn't take any baloney. He knew me – we got on pretty well – so he made do with a nod of greeting. That was enough. He didn't ask about Adam or Ibrahim. My rep was good enough to cover them.

Fat Barney's was a nightclub at night, a restaurant in the evening and a bar in the afternoon. It was pretty special whatever face it wore.

Except at ten in the morning when it had a hangover from the night before.

The cleaners were in, sprucing the place up. They worked around us till the door opened and Maldini came in. I got a pain in my gut straight from the go. Maldini had Louie Spironi with him. Spironi was dumb muscle. That meant Maldini wasn't expecting the talk to do much good. He had two other men walking behind him but they didn't interest me. They were regular hoods, easy to deal with. Spironi always worried me. Nobody should like causing hurt as much as he did.

We had taken a table near the door to the kitchens. I sat down but Adam and Ibrahim stayed on their feet. They were both armed. Ibrahim hadn't liked that but I was making the play. My rules, so he agreed.

'Take a seat,' I said to Maldini, and he dropped into the chair opposite. His guys stood behind him. They were all armed.

Maldini just looked at me. 'So?'

'What's it going to take?' I asked. 'Centurion Pictures don't need bad publicity. We don't need to be tangled in this kind of crud, especially over a nothing like Jennings. What's it going to take to persuade your boss it's over? What's the price?'

Maldini leaned forward in his chair. I could see the pockmarks on his face better, and smell last night's booze, too. 'You got the mug who stole our money?'

I didn't give a straight answer. 'If we find him, we need to know what keeps us off the front pages.'

'The boss wants his money back.'

'Fair enough,' I nodded.

Maldini wasn't done. 'Twice.'

That stopped me in my tracks. 'Twice?'

Maldini liked that he's surprised me. 'He wants double.'

'Forty big ones?' I asked. Best to be sure. I wasn't sure Maldini could count that high.

He just nodded in reply.

'That's a lot of cash,' I said.

That sick smile on Maldini's face got a bit wider. 'That's not all.'

'More?'

'He wants,' Maldini stretched it out, 'he wants an apology.'

'From me?' That wasn't happening.

'From Jennings,' Maldini answered sharpish. 'In person.'

'And how many broken bones will be involved in this apology?'

Malidini play-acted like he was offended. 'Please. Nothing to crude.' Then he gave up the act. 'Louie is an artist.'

Louise Spironi squared his shoulders and gave an ugly smile.

'And he enjoys his art too,' I said.

Maldini spread his hands, all calming like. 'He's a Biblical man. He believes in an eye for an eye.'

'Shakespeare fan as well?' Adam asked. 'He looks like he enjoys his pound of flesh.'

Louie bit on that line. 'You calling me fat?'

'No,' Adam said slowly, 'it's a reference to The Merchant of Venice.'

Louise shrugged. 'Never met the guy.'

'I don't suppose you would have,' Adam answered.

I didn't like that kind of chat between two people who weren't the main players in the meeting. I was distracting and could lead to things getting out of hand. I reigned it in, straight to business. 'So, you want forty Gees, and Ygor here gets to beat the pulp out of a guy who's ninety pounds soaking wet?'

Maldini grimaced some. 'Actually I was being more literal.'

I was surprised me knew that word "literal". It took a beat to get what he meant. *Jesus*. 'An eye for an eye?' I asked.

Maldini pursed his lips like he was talking about nothing at all. 'He might see a straighter path with just the one eye.'

Ibrahim looked disgusted. Adam just sounded angry. 'That's a heavy price to pay.'

A shrug from Maldini. 'Lessons got to be learned.'

Ibrahim's voice came now, cold and brittle. 'You don't think losing his career, being broke and terrified will teach him something?'

It had no effect on Maldini. 'I think our way will teach him more.'

Ibrahim shook his head. 'If we find him you get the forty grand but you don't get the man.'

Maldini looked like there was a bad smell in the room. 'You let him speak?' He sneered at Ibrahim. 'You get me a drink, boy, and let the real folks speak.'

Ibrahim was pissed but it was Adam who spoke. 'You talk to my friend like that again and I might do something mean, and not get between him and you.'

'Do I look scared?'

I took that one. 'No, I don't think you're smart enough for that.'

Yeah, that got his attention back onto me. He knew me. He

knew my reputation. 'You think I'm dumb?'

'I don't give you that much thought,' I said back.

'Give me the director.'

I shrugged. 'If we…'

The son of a bitch interrupted me. 'I know you have him. I know he's at your studio. I know you took him there this morning.'

He just let that hang in the air for a minute.

'Do you?' was the best I could manage. It was as weak a defence as I knew it sounded. How could the bastard know all of that?

'Not so stupid now, huh?' Yeah, he was smug now.

'I didn't say that.' I tried not to look like he just got a leg up on me.

'We'll make a swap,' Maldini said, all reasonable. 'We get the dough and the cheater and you get your buddy back.'

What the hell was he talking about? 'Buddy? I…'

They poured in through the kitchen door. Fat Barney protested at the bar and wore the barrel of a pistol across his cheek. He went down hard.

Maldini suddenly had a dozen thugs and we were outnumbered. Two of his men grabbed Adam and held him tight. He struggled, put one down with a kick to the groin. An avalanche of punches put him down and they used their shoes for added effect before dragging him back to his feet. A hard punch to the gut would have doubled him over if they hadn't been holding him up.

Ibrahim and me? We had guns pointed at our guts and if we'd moved at least one of us would have been dead.

Maldini pointed at the door his men had come through. 'Get him out of here.' They dragged Adam away.

We didn't move. There was nothing we could do.

'An exchange,' Maldini said. 'You get your pretty boy back when we get the forty gees and the director. No more negotiation.' A real nasty smile appeared on his face. 'Be a real shame if Louie had to make a mess of his pretty face.'

I wanted to kill him.

I did nothing.

We waited till Maldini and his men had gone before heading

back to the studio.

ANDY

Lisa Stone went apeshit when we told her she was directing the new movie. Actually she went apeshit twice. First time was panic and fury – why the hell had we done that to her? – and the second time was with happiness when she realised she was going to be Centurion's first female director. Honest to the possibly non-existent-god-that-I-don't-believe-in-but-I'm-hedging-my-bets-here, I have never seen a woman quite so excited about work.

When Ibrahim and Stone got back, Erimem went a different shade of batshit, and I swear I have never seen her so angry before. She listened to what Stone and Ibrahim said. I thought she was going to lose it at them for letting Adam be taken but there's a switch in her head where she goes from my goofy pal to the leader of the known world. It was a lot like that. She went from terrified girlfriend to general in the blink of an eye. It's as scary as hell when she does that. No, *she* is as scary as hell when she does that.

'Of course there was nothing you could have done.' She was in the room with us physically but her mind was thinking, looking for options, planning.

I'd been thinking too. 'How did the mob guy know Jennings was here?'

'I was thinking the same,' Erimem said.

'So was I,' Stone agreed. 'I think I know.'

'As do I,' Erimem agreed.

I was going to ask but the answer was kind of obvious.

STONE

'How much did they pay you?'

Milt shrank away from his desk. He tried to pretend that he didn't but he really did flinch badly. 'What are you talking about?'

'You betrayed us,' Erimem snapped. 'You betrayed your employer and you betrayed Adam.' Her hand was way too close to Milt's letter opener for my liking, so I took over. She had already kicked his door in. I figured I was entitled to do the same to his teeth.

'Listen, ass-hole,' I said. 'You were the only person we told Jennings was here on the lot.'

Andy added, 'And you used the name Maldini when nobody had actually mentioned him.' They were all sharp. They knew their stuff.

Milt got even paler than usual. That was saying something. I've seen snow with more color. 'I don't know what you're talking about.'

He didn't sound like even he believed it.

'What was the deal, Milt?' I asked. 'You either answer me or her.' I nodded towards Erimem. She looked ready to go over Milt's desk and tear him apart.

Something in Milt resisted the idea that a woman would be violent. Then he looked in her eyes and he broke.

'It's the only way to keep the studio out the papers over this.'

'You're in showbiz, you twat.' That was Andy. I had to ask her later about "twat". 'You're supposed to love publicity.'

'Not scandal. You know what scandal did to Fatty Arbuckle's career.'

That was a fact. Arbuckle had been accused of forcing himself on women. Or had it been a murder? Might have been both. Whatever it was, it had killed his career.

'So you're protecting the studio?' I asked. 'Protecting the studio by letting them kill one of your directors?'

'He's not a very *good* director.' Jesus, that even stopped me and Erimem for a second.

'And you are not a very good person,' Erimem said slowly.

Milt just shrugged. 'I'm a producer. What do you expect?'

Erimem was cold. 'I expect you to have twenty thousand pounds...'

'Dollars,' Andy corrected.

Erimem nodded. 'Yes, twenty thousand dollars ready, and then you will telephone your new friends. Tell them we will give them what they want.'

'What?' Yeah, that yelp was from me.

Erimem ignored me. 'Tell them they can have Jennings,' she said.

ANDY

Okay, I didn't expect that.

Well, I didn't expect my best friend to be a time travelling pharaoh with a nice bum either but I didn't expect her to be up for handing Jennings over to the Mob. Don't get me wrong, Jennings is a weasely little shitehawk, but handing him over to be tortured and possibly killed?

I suppose it made sense. Back in her time anyway. Back then they'd probably have staked him out in the desert to be munched by lions or jackals or something. Adam was innocent in this. He had gone along to back up Stone but it wasn't his fight. I was kind of disappointed that Erimem would let the Mob have Jennings but she had made her decision. She started talking about her plan.

The exchange was set for high noon.

Okay, it wasn't, but you kind of wanted it to be, didn't you?

Centurion wasn't the biggest studio in Hollywood but it did have some standing sets. There were a couple of fairly contemporary street scenes for their gangster pictures, and a couple of really good western streets. When we got there I wished Duke was wish us. Did I mention that John Wayne is an old pal of ours? See that thing on the floor? That's the name I just dropped.

The streets were usually pretty much just the fronts of buildings with little spaces behind the windows painted to look like rooms but a few buildings were more complex than that. One of the saloons, the *Tumbling Dice* actually had a saloon behind the swingy doors. One of the hotels had a lobby and a few pokey hotel rooms up on the first floor. They all shared a veranda, which seems weird. That's a burglar's paradise surely? I'm reading too much into this, aren't I?

We knew the lot from the first time we made a movie. We'd been total geeks, looking around, getting to know the place. She had made her decision about where to meet with Peterman's men pretty quickly. It was the western street that had most recently been the setting for Bucky Carson's *Silver Boom Town*. Bucky was athletic but he wasn't much of an actor. Nobody cared. He wasn't paid to act, just to look like an action star. They'd finished filming a few days earlier so the lot was abandoned.

We stood in the middle of the dusty street. Stone, me and Erimem stood out there with Milt. He looked like he wanted to be anywhere but there. I didn't blame him.

The exchange was set for three o'clock. We were there at two thirty. Erimem and I had changed into jeans and comfortable shirts. Lisa had been scandalised at the thought of Erimem just wearing her leggings. It was obscene for a young woman to just wear pantyhose, apparently. We didn't have time to debate it so comfy tight stretchy jeans it was. Oh, and *khopesh* fighting daggers for when it got boisterous.

Stone checked his watch for the third time.

'They will be here,' Erimem said calmly.

'And if they don't come?' Milt squeaked.

She didn't even look at him. 'I will slice you open from crotch to throat and let the birds feed on you while you are still alive.'

If he'd wet himself on the spot I wouldn't have been surprised. His knees dipped at what she'd said and he appealed to Stone. 'She can't do that. This is America. I've got rights.'

'So did the young guy you sold out to Peterman,' Stone shot back. He liked Adam. Probably some brotherhood of cops stuff in there, but also, two good guys with similar experiences who just got along. 'Might as well tell you, since your day is already shot,' Stone continued, 'these people aren't just actors. They're British Military Intelligence agents.'

Milt went from milk white to grey. 'Spies?'

'Something like that,' Stone agreed.

'Something,' I nodded.

Stone kept going. 'So you sold out the wrong guy, Milt.'

'I didn't sell anybody out,' the producer babbled. 'I'm just protecting the studio and the boss.'

Stone wasn't buying that. 'I bet the boss doesn't know a thing about handing Jennings over.' Milt just looked at his feet and couldn't answer. That said it all. 'I didn't think so.'

'He didn't need to know,' Milt whined.

Stone shook his head in disgust. 'You're something, Milt. I'm just not sure what.' He spat in the dirt and stared at that rather than look at the producer.

'They're here.' Erimem had straightened up and tilted her head.

I didn't see anything ahead, but then I caught it. There was dust moving from behind the façade at the end of the street. They were almost there. A few seconds later a bunch of hoods came into sight. Adam was being pushed along by a pack of goons. They could only have been Mob stooges. One was a cheap thug trying to make a cheap suit look expensive with bright flourishes like a red handkerchief in the breast pocket. That was the one Stone called Maldini. The rest were dumb muscle in dull suits. All except one. He was ugly. Everything about him was rotten. His suit was fine but it looked wrong on him, like it didn't belong, like it just didn't want to be there. He was muscular, not very tall and his face and hands had scars that could only have come from fights. When he pushed Adam there was enjoyment in it. He liked hurting people. I guessed that was the Louie Spironi Stone had warned us about. I understood the warning. Spironi was bad news. It was written all over him.

Adam had some blood coming from his nose but his face hadn't been beaten too badly. The way he walked said they had worked on his body, though.

Stone already had a big, nasty pistol in his hand. He waited until they were about ten metres away when he spoke. 'That's close enough.'

Maldini indicated for his stooges to stop. 'Where's the dough and where's the chicken?'

I held up a canvas bag. 'I've got the money.'

'And the director?'

'Why do you want him?' Erimem asked. 'What will you do with him?'

Maldini looked at her like she was dirt. He'd had disdain when he looked at me. It was worse with Erimem. So... misogynist and racist. Arsehole. 'Why does it matter to you?' he sniped.

'He has betrayed you and he tried to betray us,' Erimem said, 'but he does not deserve to die.

Yeah, Maldini had already dismissed her as a weak little girlie. 'I guess we disagree about that.'

Erimem didn't stop though. 'Milt betrayed us. Should he die also?'

'Do I look like I care?' Maldini looked bored by the question.

But Erimem wasn't ready to let it go. 'No, but we do,' she said, scrutinising Maldini closely. 'Is killing Jennings your employer Peterman's idea or is it just a chance for you to have some fun? You have the look of a man with no soul. You would enjoy it.'

Stone interrupted. 'Has to be your boss, Peterman,' he said. 'You wouldn't dare kill him without the boss's say so. You ain't got the guts for that.'

Maldini laughed off the insult. 'The boss said to ice him. The torture is my treat to the boys.'

'Yeah,' Stone said, 'Erimem's right. You'd enjoy that.'

Mention of her name brought Erimem back into the conversation. 'If you have hurt my...' she caught herself, 'our friend, there will be nowhere you can hide from me.'

'Why would I hide from a little thing like you?' Why did men in this era not see what was so blatantly obvious to most of us?

'Well,' I said, 'that's the stupidest thing you ever said.'

'Watch your mouth,' Maldini snapped. He really didn't like being talked down to by women. Tough shit. 'Where's the director?' he asked.

Stone waved a hand and Ibrahim brought Milt out onto the veranda of the hotel. Jennings' hands were tied and he looked terrified. Ibrahim looked a lot meaner than I had ever seen him before. It suited him.

'We swap the money for Adam and then you get Jennings,' Stone said.

Maldini shook his head obstinately. 'No way.'

'We do not trust you,' Erimem said flatly. 'We get Adam back before you take Jennings.'

Maldini smirked. 'And if I say no?'

Erimem rubbed her thumbs over her fingertips. She was ready to fight. 'Then I will have no choice,' she said evenly. 'I will have to come and get him.'

Maldini really didn't get it. 'Oh, I like feisty. They fight so much more.'

'You have no idea how I fight,' Erimem said. She'd shifted her weight forward onto the balls of her feet. She was set and ready.

That meant it was my time to offer some distraction. 'Is this a dick swinging contest or are we making the swap?' I asked. 'If I'm keeping this money I still have time to hit the stores and spend it.'

Maldini wanted to hit me for that. It was there in his eyes. 'You try it and we'll kill you too.'

'No more threats!' Erimem snapped. 'We make the trade and then you can take Jennings.'

Stone waved me forward. 'Andy will bring the money and one of your gorillas will bring Adam. Meet in the middle.'

I waited until Erimem gave me the nod to move and I walked more slowly than I ever walked in my life. Halfway between our position and theirs I was face to face with Adam. 'How's your day going?'

He shrugged and grimaced in pain. 'So-so. Yours?'

'Not bad. Thinking about washing my hair tonight.'

'Cool,' he nodded. 'Looking forward to a shower myself.'

'Quit your yap and hand over the dough.' Yep. Maldini really did say that. Twat.

'Release Adam and she will hand over the money,' Erimem said.

That wasn't good enough for Maldini. 'She'll do it now.'

Erimem was not for backing down. 'She will do it when Adam is released.'

'Hey, "she" has a name you know,' I protested. Just a bit

more distraction. I'm not that much of a diva.

Stone gave a big sigh. 'Maldini, you're extorting money from us. Could you do it faster? We got lives to get on with.'

'I'm extorting money from you for Mr Peterman,' Maldini corrected him. 'He told me I could enjoy myself doing it.'

'Did he tell you to be boring?' Stone asked. 'Let's get on with it.'

'Let the man go,' Erimem said slowly and carefully.

'Hand over the money.'

Erimem nodded slowly and I lobbed the bag of cash towards Maldini. 'Here. And don't spend it all in one place.'

He waved one of his goons forward to pick the nag up. 'Bring it here.'

While they grabbed the cash, I helped Adam back towards Erimem and Stone. 'Are you okay?' I asked him quietly.

Adam winced again. 'Been better,' he said through gritted teeth. 'You know some people think us Scots are bad tempered and bear a grudge?'

'Never heard it but… whatever.'

He looked back over his shoulder at Maldini and his thugs. 'Before we leave 1940 I'm going to kick the shite out of some of those bastards.'

We had reached our guys. Erimem allowed herself a moment of concern. 'Are you hurt?'

'A few bruises,' Adam answered. 'You shouldn't give Jennings up for me.'

She looked past him to Maldini. 'We are dealing with it,' she said quietly.

As for Maldini, he ha the bag and was pleased with the contents. 'Okay, I got the dough. Now where's the director? Louie needs his fun.' On cue, Louie Spironi gave a nasty laugh and lumbered forward.

'You're going to murder him, aren't you?' Erimem demanded.

'Well, we ain't gonna dance the polka,' Maldini said, sour as you like.

'What language is that you're speaking?' I called. 'Fluent gibberish?'

'Watch your mouth,' Maldini snapped. 'Yeah, we're gonna

kill him like Mr Peterman wants, and we'll enjoy doing it.'

'That's what I thoughtStone said sadly. He turned and raised his pistol. He shot three times. On the saloon veranda, Jennings jerked violently and clutched at his chest. His eyes went wide and he toppled over the wooden rail, landing in the straw cart below. We just stared at Stone.

'What are…' I struggled with the words. 'What did you do?'

Stone looked bleak, like a man who had just shot his own dog. 'It was for the best. You know they were going to kill him. Better for it to be quick than for them to torture him.'

'That wasn't the deal,' Maldini shrieked.

'You said you wanted him,' Stone answered. 'You didn't say nothing about alive. You can take him now if you want – but Crazy Louie there won't get his fun.'

Spironi reacted badly to being called crazy. 'Maybe I'll get it from you, Stone.'

There was a weird sound a sort of wind wailing. It took me a minute to realise what it was.

Maldini recognised it, too. 'Cops! You sold us out, Stone.'

'Would I shoot Jennings if I was going to call the cops?'

'Then who did?' Maldini yelped.

There wasn't time for an answer. It all went to hell. Four police cars turned into that western street giving full beans to their version of the blues and twos. They skidded to a stop in the dirt and uniforms spilled out. Maldini's men scattered, trying to run for it.

Stone went for Maldini. He was small and fast but Stone was quicker than he looked. He caught Maldini's tie in his left hand and used it to pull the weasel onto a right hand that would have flattened an elephant. It flattened Maldini's nose. Blood sprayed onto the sand. Maldini staggered and Stone hit him again.

One of the thugs tried to run past me. I pushed Milt into him and they went down in a heap. I put him out with a kick from my boot. Right foot. Dennis Bergkamp would have been proud of that shot. If you don't know who he is, I'm not sure we can be friends. Come on the Arsenal!

The nasty-looking thug was trying to run as well. Adam tackled him and brought him down, but when they got up, Louie Spironi had a nasty looking knife in his hand. He stabbed it towards Adam who skipped back a step.

Erimem eased past Adam. She had her khopesh daggers in her hands. The way she held them said she was ready for a fight. 'If you run, I may choose not to open your belly to the sun.'

STONE

'If you run, I may choose not to open your belly to the sun.'

That was when Louie Spironi made his mistake. That was when he picked a fight with Erimem.

She gave Louie the chance to run and he didn't take it. He wanted to get away, but he wanted to hurt somebody too. He couldn't resist the chance to carve this mouthy broad.

His knife was dull. The edge was sharp but it hadn't been cleaned properly since before the Talkies. There was blood and I didn't want to think what else on the blade.

'Let the police catch him,' Adam said.

He knew he was wasting his breath.

'Looking forward to cutting you open,' Louie sneered.

'I owe a kick in the teeth,' Adam answered. 'I'll take him.'

Erimem moved just enough to stop Adam from confronting Louie. 'No. This is mine.'

She took a step towards Louie. He laughed at the way she held the daggers. I just thought "You dumb bastard" and waited for him to move. He stabbed at her stomach. She moved like a dancer, moving to the side and forward, one dagger slicing upwards, the other slashing down. Both found their mark on Louie's arm, cutting through the jacket, the shirt and his skin. The torn material turned red real quick.

'Bitch!'

Erimem shook her head to stop Adam in his tracks. 'I have been called worse by better men than this... nothing.' Jeez, I never heard so much contempt in a voice before. This guy was dirt to her. She wasn't worried about him at all.

'I'll cut you apart, bitch.'

He stabbed again, this time following it with a swing of his giant paw. She ducked under his arm, twisted, spun and dragged both daggers across his thigh. He attacked again. She danced away and opened his other arm. Ever seen a cat toy with a mouse before the kill? This was it. Louie changed tack. He charged straight at her. This time she didn't back away or dodge – she went straight at him. At the last minute she grabbed his arm and used it as leverage to jump up and slam her knee into his jaw, before dropping lightly to the side and circling him.

That was when I saw it in Louie's eyes. For a decade he had terrified everybody he met. All those years as Peterman's enforcer and torturer, he'd been used to people being terrified by the thought of Louie Spironi. It dawned on him that she wasn't scared. Somewhere in his slow, dumb brain, Louie realised that he was in trouble. She wasn't afraid, she was faster than him and she was a better fighter than him. Yeah, Louie realised he was deep in trouble and he had no idea how to get out of it. Another lunge was easily avoided and two more gashes opened on his arm. Rage took over. He screamed and went at her again. This time she left him grabbing air while she took both daggers down his back. Just for a second his knees dipped like a boxer who had been caught with a hard shot to the chin. She went for the kill. One dagger slashed down across his wrist. He dropped his knife. He'd lost control of his fingers. The daggers were still moving, slicing down his forehead and across his cheek, leaving a crimson X that would live on his face as a scar for the rest of his days. His knees buckled and I thought it was over.

Louie Spironi was just too dumb for his own good. His one good hand moved for his fallen knife.

'I'll kill you.'

Erimem answered Louie's threat with speed you wouldn't believe. One hand lashed out, slamming the hilt of her dagger into his eye. The one on the side daggers had just carved open. Louie screamed and fell, grabbing his face. It didn't take Einstein to know that eye was never going to be the same again.

'You won't even see me.'

The daggers disappeared into sheaths on her back and she

turned to Adam. 'Do you need a doctor?'

'I'll see Helena in a minute,' Adam answered. 'Something I need to do first.' He kicked Louie hard in the nuts. Really hard. Pretty sure every guy who saw it felt sick and felt their eyes start to water. 'I owed him that,' Adam said. And then he let Erimem take his hand and we all turned to see what was going on.

The cops had rounded up all of the Peterman crew. Johnny Lynch was the detective running the show. I knew him from way back. He was ambitious. That was why I'd picked him for this.

'Jeez, somebody made a mess of Louie,' Lynch said. 'That your work, Stone?'

'It was mine,' Erimem said.

I just nodded. 'He came at her with a knife.'

Lynch had been in the job too long to ever look really surprised. He just shrugged. 'Fair enough.'

'He's a murderer.' Maldini was back on his feet. Damn, I'd made a mess of his face. His nose was spread across three different zip codes and pointed squint at a fourth. 'He shot a guy.'

Lynch looked me hard in the eye. 'What's this about, Stone? Did you shoot somebody?'

'Looks that way,' I nodded.

Over by the hotel, Ibrahim and Helena were helping Jennings out of the hay cart. The front of his shirt was crimson.

'That's the guy he murdered,' Maldini yelled.

Lynch just looked at him. 'The one who's walking over here?'

I held up my gun. 'You'll find three bullets in the wall of the hotel and bags of fake blood under his shirt.'

Lisa and Olivia had come out of a building. Through the open door we could see a film camera.

'We recorded everything that happened here,' Lisa said. 'My first directing job. The guy with the nose confessed that Peterman had sent him to kill Jennings.'

Lynch almost smiled. 'I need to see and hear that.'

'It'll be ready in an hour,' Lisa answered.

'But this is what you'll see.' Olivia held up a little metal rectangle. One side was a screen which showed Maldini's confession. In color, too. And we could hear it. Damn, these spies had some amazing gizmos.

Lynch was impressed by that little device, but more by the confession.

'Cuff him,' he said, and a mountain sized cop cuffed Maldini's hands behind his back.

'Mr Peterman won't stand for this,' Maldini protested.

The mountain cuffed his ear to shut him up.

'Once a judge sees that footage you can move on Peterman,' I said to Lynch.

Lynch shrugged. 'I got a tame judge I can call. We'll be on Peterman in an hour. This could be the biggest Mob sting in the city for ten years.'

'And all your own work,' I answered.

Lynch shrugged again. 'If you wanted the credit you should have stayed on the job.' He looked at the man-mountain. 'Take Maldini away. His face is turning my stomach. Probably should have a veterinarian look at Louie as well.'

Maldini was dragged away and a couple of cops carried what was left of Louie away.

'Is that it?' Jennings asked. 'Is it over?'

'This is the director?' Lynch asked.

'Yep,' I agreed.

Lynch grabbed Jennings by the collar. 'Got some questions to ask you about twenty grand being stolen.'

'What?'

Jennings was taken away in handcuffs, whining as he went. He'd be released without any charge but he'd have to disappear out of LA and the movies for a long time. At least till Peterman was in jail.

Somebody else was trying to disappear.

'Going somewhere, Milt?'

'Just going back to my office.' The producer was trying to just be anywhere else.

I decided to help him. I grabbed his collar and hurried him along. 'No need for that, Milt. You got the rest of the day off. In fact, you got the rest of forever off.'

'What?' the producer squeaked.

'He's just fired your ass,' Adam said sourly.

'He can't do that! He's just muscle!'

Lisa moved fast as a whip. 'Wrong. He's *all* muscle.' It's a really nice thing when your wife turns Lone Ranger and comes to your defence. She gave me that smile. 'Throw him out, hon.'

Who am I to disagree with my wife?

I dragged Milt through the lot, along the alley between the sound stages, past actors and directors, past my security guys until I shoved him through the gates out onto the sidewalk.

I turned round and found I had an audience clapping. Lisa, Erimem and the rest had followed me. I gave them my best bow.

'Okay,' Lisa said. 'That's enough praise. He's not used to it.'

'Come on,' Helena said. 'Let's make movies.'

CHAPTER SIXTEEN

It was weird relaxing into life in 1940 Hollywood, knowing that over in Britain and in Europe, war was raging. It was maybe more interesting to see how America was reacting to the war. Some wanted to stay out of it, some wanted to get involved. I hated knowing that they would be up to their necks in it by the end of 1941.

Adam recuperated and we got on with making the film. It was hard work, the days were long and we didn't exactly have twenty takes on any scenes, but we didn't need them. Lisa Stone turned out to be a really good director. *Yeah, like I know anything about that!* But, she did get things moving and she got the action scenes looking good. She got us rehearsing the song and dance number as well. Really wishing I'd read the script or watched the film properly before handing it across. I could have excised that dancing bit.

At lunch on the first Sunday of filming it was just the seven of us. Rosa was away at church, probably praying for us godless heathens. Which was nice of her. She had left a cold lunch, which was fine.

Olivia and I had decided to spill the beans about us living together full time. I don't know what I had expected. Part of me is still wary – not about being gay but about how people are going to react. These people were the family I'd picked for my life but I was still a bit wary. At least until the hugs started. Lots of smiles, lots of hugs, lots of congratulations. Even Tom was pretty genuine. I think he was starting to relax into the 40s. He's started wearing a fedora.

Helena handed out the wine. Good wine. 'So where are you going to live? And when?'

'The future,' Olivia answered. 'Not this time. The *future* future. Your time.'

'We know what you mean,' Ibrahim said reassuringly. He's a very nice man, you know. And men are not my specialist subject. 'Are you going to live at your place?'

That was something we had talked about in bed the night before. The house I was in… that place was all about my past, the sadness that went with what happened to Mum and Dad. This felt new and fresh. I wanted to live somewhere that didn't have shadows attached to it.

'We're going to buy somewhere new. We don't know where yet, but we'll find a house.'

That confused Adam. 'I thought you were giving up the job and starting uni. Won't you struggle for money?'

Helena fielded that. 'Time travel, bank accounts opened in the past, compound interest… we're all minted.'

'Shit.' Adam sucked on the inside of his cheek. 'Is that legal?'

'Are there any laws which prohibit using time travel for financial gain?' Erimem asked.

'No.'

'She gave her royal proclamation. 'Then it is legal.'

Adam wasn't finished. 'But what about papers? Birth certificates, national insurance…'

Ibrahim took over. 'We had that problem with Erimem. 'We faked it up. A few fibs, a few quid and the best computer in the world built her a history. We'll do the same for Olivia.'

'I'm a copper,' Adam said slowly. 'Are you actually telling me that you plan to forge documents?'

Helena just smiled. 'Pretty much.'

Erimem picked up a dull card security pass from a table and handed it to Adam. 'You can't complain. You also have a forged pass, saying you are an operative of Britain's secret services.'

He looked at the pass in shock. 'I should arrest the whole bloody lot of you.'

'And who would you hand us to?' Erimem asked primly.

'You have no authority here and you are holding forged documents.' She gave a cheeky smile. 'I believe that means you should also be arrested.'

Adam stared at his pass and stuffed it in his pocked. 'You're all mental, every single one of you.' There was no malice in him. I think he was pretty pleased to be in on the joke.

Helena was already thinking, though. 'You know, the house next to ours is on the market. Big, detached, nice garden...'

'And the one next to that on the end is moving, too,' Ibrahim added. 'I'm trying not to take that personally.'

'We only need one house,' I said.

'They were not thinking of you,' Erimem said.

Helena offered a little smile. 'We thought you might like a little privacy while still staying nice and close?'

Erimem thought about it for a moment. 'I know you are eager to start a family. It might be good for you to have space also.' Her nose twitched with mischief. 'And you will have privacy to start your family without interruption.'

Helena blushed and Ibrahim looked uncomfortable. There was a story to be heard there.

I thought about it for a minute. 'It might be nice if we all lived close by... nice or really weird and creepy.'

'I say "nice", I think,' Erimem said.

'Helena nodded. 'Same here.'

'You have a brother,' Adam said. 'What do you think he's going to say about this?'

Well, there was a question. 'My useless brother is a long story. He won't complain.' I took a sip of wine. 'We're buying houses,' I said to Erimem. 'How grown up are we?'

Erimem grimaced slightly. 'I must confess that I have already bought a house.' All eyes turned to her. '*This* house,' she went on. 'I like it and I like this time period. Except the underwear, that is very uncomfortable. Yes, I bought this property. The lot also included the two smaller houses next to this one.'

'When did you become a property tycoon?'

Erimem looked a bit embarrassed. 'I am uncomfortable that we are here so little but Rosa has to travel every day. I will give her use of one of the houses free of cost for the rest of her life.'

You know what? For a movie star, she's not bad.

ADAM

So, how does an Edinburgh laddie who works as a copper in That London wind up on a pirate ship 300 years ago in the middle of a battle?

You know something?

It's not that difficult.

Well, not when your girlfriend is a time traveller. Make that a time travelling ex-Pharaoh, expert warrior, 1940s movie star, who is also a student and administrator at a university in 2020s London.

And I will bet you a penny I am the only man alive who used that sentence today.

So, how did I wind up as Death's Head Docherty, Scourge of the Seven Seas, and Pirate in the Caribbean?

Here's how it happened. Andy and Olivia had given us their news. I was still coping with the fact that I was party to my girlfriend having forged documents on top of her being a time travelling pharaoh movie star warrior student. Now I had to accept that Andy was going to be living with a pirate captain from sixteen hundred and oatcake. I knew Olivia was from the past and I knew she loved Andy. You could see it when they looked at each other – and you could see how much they hated hiding it when they had to. And I was now accessory to her getting forged documents. You know what? Sod it. They're a nice couple. I like them, and more importantly, Erimem loves them both. Especially Andy. They're really close. For full disclosure's sake, I also have forged papers which say I am some kind of 1940 James Bond so I can't really nick them for anything.

Anyway… Andy and Olivia had a few things they needed to sort out. Erimem and I were in the garden, chilling by the pool. How Hollywood is that? Helena and Ibrahim had taken Rosa to do some shopping for her new house, and Tom had tagged along with them. He was trying to be less of a spare wheel, trying to fit in.

So, Her Majesty and I were relaxing by the pool when Andy and Olivia came over.

'We've got a few errands to run,' Andy said.

Erimem tilted her hat so she could see Andy. 'Shopping?'

'Business,' Andy answered. 'Long ago business.'

'My ship,' Olivia explained. 'I must give my ship to the crew and Andy has plans for my booty.'

I almost spat my beer at the expression on Andy's face.

'That was just an expression, dear,' she choked out. 'Moving swiftly on, with a reminder to expand your use of colloquialisms, we need to sort out Olivia's banking matters.'

'I understand,' Erimem said. 'Would you like us to come with you?'

Andy's nose wrinkled. 'No need. Thanks for the offer, but it should be a quick scoot back, get the wedge into the right bank, which we know will survive through to our time, arrange a few visits, say cheerio to the crew and then back here. Given that there's no real travel involved, we should be able to do it all in an hour or two.'

Olivia agreed. 'I know what I have to do.'

Andy nodded. 'I'm just going along for immoral support, and because I really fancy wearing one of those Poldarky frocks.'

'Isn't Poldark about a hundred years later than this?' I asked.

'Haven't you got a missing cat to find or something?' Andy scowled. 'And when did you become an expert on all things Poldark? You got a secret thing about romantic novels?'

'No, but I fancy Demelza.' I held up a hand. 'At least I did until I met Erimem.'

Erimem looked to Olivia. 'Do you have any idea what they are talking about?'

Olivia shook her head. 'No.'

'Neither do I,' Erimem sighed. She tipped her hat brim down and settled back onto the lounger. 'Enjoy yourselves.'

'You too,' Andy said. 'You've got the place to yourselves. Have fun. Don't do anything we wouldn't… well, anything we haven't already done.' She gave a huge cheesy grin and twisted her time travel ring. Olivia did the same and they were gone in a little storm of electricity. Never going to get used to seeing people just disappear. It's just too whacko.

Andy was right, though. 'We do have the place to ourselves.'

Erimem lifted her brim and eased her shades down her nose. 'Are you suggesting that we should go inside and…?'

I looked around the empty garden. 'Do we have to go inside?'

She pretended to be horrified. 'And if the newspapers have sent a photographer?'

'Are you really a big enough star for them to do that?'

'That is the kind of question that will lead to use not going inside.'

Okay. I admitted defeat. 'You win. You know fame better than me.' I held out a hand and pulled Erimem to her feet.

'I ruled the world,' she said. She sounded playful but it was odd to know that was true. She really had ruled a huge chunk of the world. And she had given it up.

She put her hand more comfortably in mine and we started towards the house. We'd managed about five paces before the air in front of us erupted in a ball of electricity and Andy appeared, toppling to the grass in front of us. Her olde worlde dress was turn and smeared with blood. There was blood on her face too, and a desperate look in her eyes.

'I need help.' She struggled back to her feet. 'They've got Olivia. You've got to help me get her back.'

We got Andy indoors so that she could explain what had happened.

'We'd arrived in Port Margueritte where Olivia's ship was berthed so the crew could carouse their way through every brothel in town. We had put out word for the crew to gather on the *Future's Hope*. That's the boat's name. After that we got her cash and stuff and deposited it in a bank. We just got back to Port Margueritte to tell the crew to find a new captain when we got jumped. We fought them but there were just too many of them.

Olivia was knocked unconscious. I don't know how bad she's hurt. One of the arseholes took her time travel ring. I couldn't do anything on my own.' She looked desperate. I'd never seen her like that before. It didn't sit well on her. 'You've got to help me.'

Erimem didn't bother looking to me. She didn't have to. We'd do whatever it took. 'Of course. We should go at once.'

'I'll leave a note for Helena,' I said. 'Just in case we need a doctor.'

Even under her tan I saw Andy turn pale at that thought.

Five minutes later, we were three hundred years earlier.

The past stinks. I mean it really smells. At least the harbour at Port Margeuritte does. Did. Does. Whatever. It really reeked of fish. And other stuff. The local sewage system seemed to consist of whatever wall people could hang their arses over. You know, that's not fair. The island looked... well, it looked like every Caribbean island you ever dreamed about. It was just the way you'd expect it to look. Thick vegetation, with a small town at the harbour. It was a couple of dirt streets with bars and supply stores. Other that those, various buildings were scattered about. If you've seen *Black Sails*, think that.

The biggest bar was Salty's. We'd seen three ships in the harbour and it seemed that the bulk of the three crews were in there. For the most part they seemed to be grouped by crew but enough bevvy had gone down their necks for the lines to blur at the edges and the crews start to mingle.

We had changed into clothes appropriate for the time – and I know it's wrong to say, but Erimem is definitely keeping that pirate outfit. She looked... wow. So did Andy, to be fair, but my eyes were on Erimem. We stood out in the bar because our clothes were obviously new. Actually we also stood out because our clothes were *clean*.

Andy and Erimem recognised one of the better dressed sailors.

'Mr Barron,' Andy said.

He looked relieved to see her. 'Miss Andrea. Where did you go? You told me about the skipper and then...' he recognised Erimem and things made sense to him. 'Ah... you went for help.'

'Hello, Mr Barron,' Erimem said. 'I am pleased to see you are well.'

'That I am,' Barron answered, 'but I worry for the skipper.'

'We will find her,' Erimem said confidently – and it didn't take Brian Cox to work out that was for Andy as much as Barron, 'and then we will celebrate her safe return as her enemies dance their last on a tight rope.

My girlfriend is really quite bloodthirsty. You might have noticed.

Her words certainly roused Barron. 'I've got eyes out looking and listening for any news. Meantime we did what Miss Andrea said and came here and acted like nothing had happened.'

'That is wise,' Erimem said. She was thinking like a soldier, planning her campaign. There's something on her face that changes when she turns into this warrior general. The funny-quirky-sexy just disappears and she's... she's somebody else. I saw it when I found out about this weird, weird life and she dragged me into the future. It's really unsettling to see. She was still talking quietly. 'Some of the crew are talking with other sailors.'

'My smartest lads,' Barron said. 'They're finding out if these crews know anything.'

'And if they do?' I felt like I should ask something since nobody had bothered to introduce me.

Barron looked at me as if I was an idiot. 'They'll tell us what they know. Rum will see to that.'

'And the men you have out searching?' Andy asked quickly. 'I don't know everybody aboard but I know this is only half the crew.'

The crew looked at her with a mixture of recognition, relief and fear.

'We are using the supply huts as a base,' Barron said quietly before raising his voice. 'Show you the ship? Can't it wait till tomorrow? There's drink to be had today.'

Erimem answered. She caught the ruse easily enough. 'Now,' she said loudly. 'It is too long since I had timbers below my feet.'

Fair play to her, she had all the lingo. I bet she's see the *Pirates of the Caribbean* films. Even the duff ones. Barron made a show of taking us out to see the ship. We wandered along towards the harbour before taking a sharp turn and winding up in a wooden building that was really just a glorified shed with a dirt floor. The sailors in there looked nervously at Erimem.

'Why are they so scared of you?' I asked.

'She killed their last captain, Andy answered absently.

Erimem wasn't sure how I'd react. 'He was not a good captain,' she said defensively. 'He murdered many people and tried to kill us all.'

'Enough history.' Andy went straight to the nearest sailor. 'Do you have any idea what happened to Olivia?'

He shook his head. 'Didn't find anything.'

A few more crewmen echoed his lack of success, but then the big wooden doors were shoved open. I swear to the god I don't believe in that he had an eyepatch. He was out of breath and agitated. 'Other side of the island,' he gasped. 'The skipper's being taken to a ship at anchor on the other side of the island.'

'Show us,' Erimem said quickly. She turned to the rest of the men. 'All of you come with us.'

'Except one,' Barron interrupted. 'Tanner, go and get the rest of the crew. Tell them where we're going.'

A thought occurred to me. 'What if they're involved? The other crews, I mean.'

Eyepatch shook his head. 'I recognised the ship. The flag anyway. It's Lescal. The *Marseille* is the only ship with that flag.'

'Lescal?' Andy sounded concerned by the name. 'Olivia's mentioned him. He's bad news. Really bad.'

'He is that,' Barron confirmed. 'Lescal is a killer. He's the most feared privateer in these waters. Even other pirates avoid him.'

'So what would he want with Olivia?' Andy demanded.

'The last few months have been good,' Barron answered. 'We raided a pair of big Dutch ships, a couple of English Merchantmen and…' That was when it clicked for him. 'We took a ransom not to attack a French envoy's ship. He was an important man. He didn't like paying us. The skipper had a suspicion he might take some revenge.'

Somebody had to ask. 'And what would that revenge be?'

Barron didn't want to answer. 'Maybe a trial. Maybe just

straight to execution.'

Erimem caught Andy before she could react to that. 'That will not happen to Olivia. We will not let that happen.'

Andy just nodded. I saw Erimem give Andy's arm a squeeze before she turned to Barron. 'We must move faster. We have to catch them.'

'You heard her, dogs,' Barron bellowed at his sailors. 'Keep up or the skipper will have the skin off your backs.'

I have to admit, I didn't think that would have encouraged me to save Olivia. Save her so she can flay the skin off my back? You know what? I'll leave her where she is, thanks. But the sailors picked it up and hurried through the thick undergrowth. Within half an hour we'd caught up with a party of sailors heading for a boat pulled up onto the cleanest beach you've ever seen. There was no sign of Olivia with them.

'Shit.' That came from Andy. She pointed out to sea. Halfway between the beach and a ship that seemed to have a cannon at every window there was another boat being rowed towards the ship. It was rolling a bit and there was some kind of stremash going on in it. It didn't take long to recognise that Olivia was fighting like a wild thing. She was punching and kicking anything she could reach. I'm not surprised. I didn't want to think what a crew of bastards like that would do to a bonnie lass like Olivia before handing her over.

I could tell that was exactly what Andy was thinking about.

We took Lescal's men when they moved out of view of the beach behind some twisted weird looking trees. We were on them from nowhere. They didn't stand a chance. It didn't stop us hitting them hard. Some of them died in a fight that lasted less than a minute. The rest were battered into a quick submission. The brutality of it… look, I've seen a fair bit as a copper but there was no law here. It didn't come into anybody's thinking. This was just what these sailors felt they had to do. I can't lie. I wasn't comfortable with it. But I'd have been more uncomfortable with them getting away with Olivia.

'Get their clothes and hats,' Erimem said. 'Their friends will recognise the clothes.'

The injured and the dead were both stripped and eleven of us pulled on their clothes. The rest of the crew waited for orders.

Once they were given, we were on our way, dressed in stolen clothes. Olivia was keeping the other boat too busy for them to pay any attention to us.

By the time we pulled up alongside the Marseille, Olivia had already be dragged up onto the deck. Erimem had to hold Andy back to stop her charging up the ropes and ruining the whole thing. We could all hear Olivia's voice yelling up on deck and these damn pirates tormenting her. If it had been Erimem up there King Kong couldn't have stopped me going up.

Things sounded bad on deck. The further up the ropes we got the worse they sounded. Olivia was yelling, screaming and cursing.

She was surrounded by a good dozen of them. They were grabbing at her, pushing her, yanking at her hair. One of them was a vile, filthy of turd. Two black teeth in his head but an evil look in his eye. He was holding out Olivia's time travel ring, taunting her with it.

'You want it back. What will you give me for it? What will you do for it?'

Olivia grasped for the ring desperately but she was too slow. The ham of a hand closed around it. She looked round, desperately searching for a weapon, a way off deck. She spotted us coming up onto deck quietly but give her credit, she didn't linger on us. She focused on the ugly bastard with the black tusks.

'I will tell you precisely what I will give you,' she said haughtily. 'I will give you your life.'

Tusker laughed and sprayed spit as he did. 'You can give me something better than that, girlie.' His hands reached for her and I knew he wasn't getting off this boat alive.'

'You have something that does not belong to you.' Erimem's voice was clear and strong.

Every pair of eyes turned at us in shock. That was the element of surprise gone.

Erimem continued, 'Release her and none of you need die here.'

Some of the Marseille's crew looked shocked, others looked like they wanted to flay the skin off us.

'You get one chance,' Erimem said slowly. 'One chance

only. Let her go.'

Tusk and his friends were getting past their surprise at seeing us on their ship. They were realising that they outnumbered us by a hell of a lot.

'More girls to go round,' Tusk said. He thrust his hips at Erimem and Andy.

Andy didn't hold back. 'Give it a rest, you bloated perv. You'd never find it under the layers of blubber.'

A couple of the crew laughed at Tusk, but didn't think it was funny. 'I'm breaking you first,' he threatened Andy.

'The only thing you'd break is the bathroom scales.' Andy looked at Olivia. 'Are you okay?'

'So far.'

I don't know Olivia that well. She's usually quite quiet. Maybe it's because I'm a copper. Maybe it's because I'm new to their group. She had big brass bollocks, though, standing there ready to fight these bastards off.

Tusk was speaking again. 'She won't be. None of you will once we've had out fun.'

Erimem pulled her fighting daggers. 'If you touch her again I will open your belly and throw you to the sharks.'

Tusk wasn't too bothered. 'There's a lot more of us than there is of you.'

He was right about that. But not as much as he thought. While we had climbed up the rope onto the ship, the men we'd kept out of sight on the floor of the boat quietly went round to the other side and had climbed aboard there. There were still more of them than of us but we had surprised and we had them trapped in the middle, so we had a chance. That had been Erimem's plan. It wasn't exactly *Operation Overlord* but she'd had all of thirty seconds to come up with it.

We didn't have time to think about it. As soon as Erimem said 'But we have you surrounded' we were into a battle. There were a few pistols and they bloody near exploded every time they fired. Anyone who was hit went down. A shot to the arm or leg probably meant amputation if it got near the bone. These lead ball weren't like our bullets. If the lead balls hit bone they shattered it completely and the limb probably had to come off.

A couple of these pirates – on both sides – were going to be sporting hooks and peg legs before long. They screamed as the pistols fired. Every one sounded like a wee explosion. And then the high pitched scream. Once the gunfire was done it was swords and knives at close quarters. If you didn't have a weapon – and I didn't – we used our fists. The police training came in useful. The nearest pirate came at me with a knife. I did what the instructors had taught me and I sent him over the side into the water. I didn't have time to look for the next one. He was already coming at me. I grabbed one of the big wooden pegs used for securing ropes – belaying pins I found out they're called – and used that like a baton. I cracked him across the skull and he went over the side as well. In the few moments that had taken the deck had turned into a battleground. The pirates tried to break free from the middle of the deck but our forces came at them from both sides. Blood spattered the deck making it slippy and almost impossible to move on without skidding. Somehow, Andy and Erimem were managing it. They were making a bee-line for Tusk, who gripped Olivia by the arm. He lifted a knife to threaten her. One of Erimem's daggers flashed end over end through the air, catching the light as it went before slamming into Tusk's neck. He just looked surprised and then dropped to the deck. Andy grabbed Olivia in a huge hug. That was it for their reunion. Erimem was dragging them towards the side of the boat. It really wasn't much of a plan. Sneak aboard, rush the crew, get Olivia away and then swim like buggery. Or row like buggery, if you were on the boat. She looked for me, caught my eye, nodded that it was time to go and then her eyes widened. She pulled her hand back and threw the other dagger. I didn't have time to move. It was flying straight at my face.

Straight past my face. *Just.*

There was a sickening sound as it speared into the forehead of a pirate who had hid cutlass lifted, ready to kill me. Straight through the skull into the brain.

I didn't have time to thank her. A wooden door slammed open. I swear to god it was like a gunshot. And there he was. No doubts. That was the pirate captain Lescal. His men were terrified of him but they were relieved to see. Suddenly they couldn't lose. You could see it in them. They grew a foot taller with confidence.

'What have we here?' Lescal asked in a drawling French accent. 'Someone is trying steal my prize?' He recognised some of the sailors and focused on Barron. 'You are loyal but stupid, Barron. The ship was yours. With her gone, you could be captain. Now you are just dead.' His eyes found Olivia, and beside her Erimem and Andy. 'Or did you bring us more entertainment for my men? They look fresh. We will change that. My men will make old hags of them by morning.'

I knew Erimem would react to that. I wanted to tell her not to, to keep quiet, but that's not who she is. She pushed one of Lescal's men aside so she stood about four or five feet in front of the pirate. 'I doubt if any of you could satisfy a woman.' She pointed at Lescal's hand. On the little finger of the right hand was the familiar shape of the time travel rings we all wore. Lescal had claimed it. 'You wear a woman's jewellery.'

'A prize. I took it.'

Erimem lifted her hand showing the travel ring she always wore on her thumb. 'Try to take mine, if you have the courage.'

Lescal laughed. 'Brave girl. I save her for myself. I have fun breaking her.'

Erimem's eyebrow lifted. 'The only thing you can break is wind. You stink.'

I didn't know what she was doing but she was up to something and I trusted her.

'I break you here in front of my men.' Lescal reached for her...

Erimem twisted her time travel ring and she was surrounded by a ball of electricity. She disappeared.

And so did Lescal's outstretched arms.

He stared at the smouldering stumps where his arms used to be. The smell of overcooked meat drifted across the deck. Everybody just stared for a moment.

Then a familiar voice came from the upper deck where the wheel was, where the officers usually stood.

'Put down your weapons.'

Erimem leaned casually on the rail. She was holding Lescal's neatly amputated hands. She removed the time travel ring and pocketed it before tossing the hands towards Lescal. Instinctively he tried to reach out and catch them – but only really realised he had nothing to catch them with when they dropped by his stumps onto the deck.

Erimem gave a wry smile. 'I should have known you would need a hand to catch those.'

Lescal screamed and that was the sign for his crew to panic. One of them howled 'She's a witch!' and that set them off even worse. Another shouted, 'Ships!'

Three ships had rounded the nearest spit of land and were closing on our boat, fanning out to surround it.

I looked up at Erimem and she just smiled back at me serenely. She had arranged these ships to be here. It probably had something to do with time. I wasn't going to work it out. She knew what she was doing.

Lescal's crew scrambled to get over the side. They knew they'd lost. Our own bunch of murderous cut-throats (perfect company for a police sergeant, I'm sure you'll agree) roared in victory and I followed Andy and Olivia up to join Erimem on that upper deck. Barron was close behind me.

'How did you do that?' he asked Erimem.

It was Andy who answered. 'Didn't you hear? She's a witch.'

Erimem just smiled and reached for my hand. Nothing showy. Just a feeling like that was how it should be.

'That's our ship,' Barron said. 'And the others from the harbour.'

'Don't ask,' Andy said. 'Just don't ask.' She looked Olivia square in the eyes. 'And don't scare me like that.'

'I wasn't worried,' Olivia said. 'I knew you would come for me.'

Andy grabbed Olivia and kissed her on the mouth.

Barron stared.

So did the crew.

'I think,' Erimem said slowly, 'that Olivia and Andy need to talk with you.'

Half an hour later, it was done. Olivia had handed command to Barron, the treasure from Lescal's ship had been split between the three crews who had sailed from Port Margeuritte, and we were ready to go. Lescal's ship and its treasures were now the property of all three captains and crews, except for the trinkets Barron insisted we take. The last we heard was them discussing – and arguing – about the best way for the ship to benefit all crews, maybe with a crew made up with lads from all three ships, so the plunder would be shared equally. I think we might have just turned pirates into socialists. I could almost hear Dad's approval from 300 plus years away.

Barron was fairly stunned to be captain of the ship and the crew were genuinely saddened Olivia was leaving them. Then Andy told me how much they'd made with Olivia as skipper and I understood why they didn't want her to go. Quiet wee Olivia was a bit of pirate legend, nicknamed the Scarlet Queen because of the bloody battles she won, and her departure was being kept quiet from the other crews. Barron had decided it would be best for business to recruit another young woman to pretend to be the Scarlet Queen. I think Andy nicked that idea from *The Princess Bride* and gave it to Barron. It's weird to think of a fictional pirate story influencing these real pirates. It made sense, I suppose. Their reputation was everything. Usually the opponents gave up without a fight. Keep the legend alive and they would have a cushy life. I did have to wonder about myself, though. I'm a copper. I got into the job because I believe in the law. Here I was on the side of pirates and at least party to forgery of documents for Olivia to live in the Twenty First century. The law matters. It matters to me. Even the stupid ones I don't agree with. I really wasn't comfortable with the relaxed way Erimem and her friends – now my friends too - talked about bending or breaking the law. I was going to have to come to terms with that. By this point I liked Erimem a lot. Really a lot, and I liked what was happening with us. I suppose life makes us evolve our opinions and make compromises. I knew I was ready to give some ground. I wondered if Erimem was too.

I decided to think about that later. A few hundred years later.

Erimem had given Olivia her ring back and we headed off back to the future.

The second we arrived I knew something was wrong with Erimem.

ERIMEM

It is a very strange thing to know and to love a person that you have never actually met and who may never have really existed.

I never met my grandfather and knew very little of him. He died long before I was born. However I now have memories of spending time with him as a child and a great warmth and affection for him. He has explained this to me in what I can only think of as visions, dreams in which we meet and talk. He was from the future as well as the past and lived in both times so that he could battle a great evil in the past. Andy has spent a great deal of time trying to turn all of that into a simple single sentence of explanation. Her most recent attempt is something like "Manipulative weirdy woo-woo Grandad messing with your mind", which is probably quite close to the truth. I know that he has influenced my thoughts so that I think well of him and cannot bear him ill will for doing so.

I cannot help but trust him.

On this occasion we met on a busy beach. We sat on loungers as people moved around us enjoying the sun. He wore his usual clothing, as he would in Egypt, though with a pair of sun-glasses and yet no-one seemed confused by him. In fact, no-one looked at him at all. He took a sip of a pale orange drink.

'Hello child.'

'Hello old man.'

His head tilted back to enjoy the sun and a smile stretched across his old face. 'No respect for a Pharaoh.'

'I could say the same,' I replied. I noticed that there was very little clothing on this beach, and that my grandfather's eyes were open and moving behind the dark glasses. 'I assume the topless women are why you chose this beach?'

There was no apology in his reply. 'I'm old not dead.'

'Yes, you are,' I reminded him.

'So I am.' He shrugged. 'Semantics. Anyway, I'm here because I thought you might like to see people. 2020 is such a bad year for a social life.'

'And you know I was on my way back to the 1940s,' I replied patiently.

'So I do.'

'So?' I pressed gently.

'So what?'

He was obviously in the mood to be particularly annoying. 'So why have you brought me here?' I asked patiently.

'To protect me from these women,' my grandfather laughed. 'I am irresistible. I had more than fifty wives.'

'None of whom are here,' I reminded him.

'I don't know.' He lifted his sunglasses to look at a woman who seemed to be in her late thirties. 'She could be fifty one.'

'She looks more like a thirty six to me,' I answered. 'Double D.' That was a joke Andy had used once when we were shopping. I stole it from her.

My grandfather was still not paying me a great deal of attention. 'What's that?'

'Nothing.'

'I'll believe you,' he answered,

'You always do this.' I gave him what I hoped was my stern Pharaoh look. 'You always distract me.'

'I'm good at it, too,' he chuckled.

'So why am I here?' I demanded more gently than I would with anyone else.

The old man sighed. 'You have to fix something.'

This was not a surprise to me. My grandfather usually only summoned me when there was a task requiring my attention. 'Fix what?'

'A mistake you made,' he said without looking at me.

'*I* made?' I demanded.

His face wrinkled as he realised he had to be clearer. 'Well, you as a group, but you're the one I invite inside my head.'

'I thought we were in *my* head?'

'Both,' he nodded, 'and yes, you all have caused a huge problem.'

I sighed and settled into my lounger to listen to what he had to tell me.

ANDY

'Okay, you want to run that one by me again?' I think my voice was high enough to scare dogs. 'I did what?'

'Not you,' Erimem said. She was trying to be kind. Shit, we really were in trouble. 'Well, sort of you but not really you because we all agreed to go ahead with it and when we did...'

'We caused the world to end,' I said. My mouth was as dry as a dingo's armpit. 'I caused the world to end.'

'Tell us exactly what your grandfather said.' That was Adam. He was putting his copper head on, trying to get the facts in order.

We were back in the house in 1940s LA. Helena handed me a drink. I really hoped it was a double.

Erimem sat on the sofa. 'Here is what my grandfather told me.' She sipped a glass of wine. 'The film we are making is the problem with time.'

'Everybody's a critic,' I muttered. It didn't make me feel better.

'The film was not written by anyone,' Erimem continued. 'We abandoned the script that was written and used what we found online, but we did not write it. Nobody did. As such, it should not exist at all. It is an anomaly causing a disturbance in time.' She looked me in the eye. 'Those are the correct words?'

'Sound right to me.'

'Good.' She nodded and took another sip. I had a swig of good whisky. 'The disturbance in time caused a change in history which caused the Earth to end in 1999.' My stomach lurched again. She wasn't done. 'However, we can stop this disturbance and put history back to its proper track by creating a... what did he call it? "An opposing wave" which will cancel out the wave we already created.'

There was a silence in the room for a minute before I felt like I had to say something. 'Oh, is that all?'

She missed the snark. I must be slipping. 'Yes. Apparently it is quite easy. We must only bring two artefacts from the past to this – well, this time and our time – and they will create a...' she sought the correct words, '...a harmonic resonance.' She smiled broadly. 'I have no idea what that is.'

'Did spooky Grandad tell you what the objects are?' That was Helena.

Erimem nodded. 'He also told me where they are.'

'So, let's go and get them.' Helena stopped when she saw Erimem's face. 'Okay, what's that hitch with is going to get them? Where are they?'

Erimem sighed. 'They are in the Pharaoh's royal palaces in Thebes.' She set her wine down. 'I have to go home.'

Okay, so I have been to the Pharaoh's palace in ancient Egypt before. Erimem and I went to visit her Mum. One last chance to see her mother. It's a long story and I'm not getting into it now. Just take it as read it was an important thing for both of us.

This was different.

Last time we went at it very ninja. Sneaked in, saw her mum and sneaked out. Just the two of us. This time there were five of us. Tom and Olivia had stayed behind but Helena had been desperate to see Thebes in its pomp and Ibrahim... well, he was going to see his family. And Adam? Well, if Erimem was going somewhere potentially dangerous, so was he. When your best mate starts seeing somebody you're supposed to be a bit wary and suspicious of them. Are they good enough for your amazing pal? I think she'd done okay with Adam.

The sun over Thebes was wildly hot. Brutal. Erimem and Ibrahim were both from Egypt and Helena was Greek though she'd lived in Egypt. I was relieved that they all seemed to wilt in the heat the same way Adam and I did. They'd obviously spent too long exposed to the UK's crummy weather. For Adam and me? An hour of this tops before we actually melted.

'It's incredible.' Ibrahim was completely in awe of the place.

'It's home,' Erimem said simply. She pointed at the extraordinary palace. Really sorry to the Queen (who I very much like respite my Republican leanings) but this palace absolutely dwarfed Buck House. It was vast. Enormous, stretching a hundred metres plus. Probably two or three hundred. It was so big it was impossible to gauge. It wasn't the only building either. It was a huge complex of them. Erimem pointed out barracks for the palace guard, slave quarters, stables, stores. And then she pointed to a large ornately carved temple, which was one of many temples. 'We must go to the temples. That is where they should be.'

'Where what should be?' I asked. 'You still haven't told us what we're here to pick up.'

She didn't answer. She just started towards a complex of ornate buildings she'd called temples. Priests and servants moved around going about their business, doing whatever they were doing. And I got the idea from the topless dresses some of the serving girls were wearing it was *who* they would be doing as well.

I asked, 'Are they…?'

Erimem answered, 'Hesets.'

'And the same to you.'

'No,' she wrinkled her nose. 'They are temple hesets. They… work here.'

'Hookers?' I asked.

'Not exactly.' She shrugged. 'But by the standards of your time, probably very close. Things are different here. What they do is honourable and acceptable here. It is a way of communing with the gods.'

'Damn, they must be good in bed,' I muttered.

We followed Erimem into the temple. It wasn't cold inside but it was definitely cooler and the lights came from torches burning on the walls. Statues stood everywhere and the walls were covered with paintings and carvings, many of which showed a woman in a tight Egyptian dress with a feather standing up proudly in her head dress.

'This is the Temple of Maat,' Erimem explained. She pointed to the woman with the feather sticking out of her head. 'She is the god of truth and justice. The ostrich feather she wears in her head dress represents truth.'

'If she wore it in 1940 it would represent the height of fashion,' I answered. It didn't get much of a laugh.

Ibrahim was just rapt, looking at everything inside the temple. He had seen this kind of stuff before but always when it was thousands of years old. Here it was where it belonged. He was breathing in the living history that had always fascinated him. He was completely lost in the place. Helena just had a sort of indulgent look on her face, loving to see how much he loved it. She was taking joy from his joy. It was just really beautiful to see.

Adam? He was still just shadowing Erimem, there if she wanted him for anything, but mostly letting her have her time with her thoughts here. I decided to kill the stupid jokes for a while. This had to be weird and emotional for her so I gave her some space. She was lost in memories of this place. I let her have her time with them.

Eventually her eyes focused and she started moving towards an alcove where there seemed to be offerings of food and livestock to a statue of Maat, who didn't look all that appreciative, to be honest.

'They should be here,' Erimem said.

'What should?' Helena asked. She had left Ibrahim behind to join Erimem by the statue.

'Two gold rings,' Erimem said. 'This statue wore then, one on each hand to show that she was balanced and fair.' She pointed at the little fingers of the hands. 'She wore them on the outer fingers of either hand.'

'So where are they?' I asked. 'Where are the rings?'

'That is a question I have asked many times,' a deep, rich voice thundered from behind us. 'Though I have yet to find an acceptable answer. I wonder if five strangers skulking in Pharaoh's palace might have the answer.'

A huge bull of a man in his late forties was standing behind up, a sword in his hand. He had a military uniform that was ornate enough to say he was an officer – a high ranking one at that. Safe to say he was not happy to see us.

'Strangers?' Erimem's voice was playful and warm. She turned from the statue and fixed the soldier with the biggest smile you could ever imagine. 'I have been gone for some time but I did not think my noble Antranak would ever call me a stranger.'

He dropped his sword. He almost dropped to his knees in shock. I swear to whatever god you believe in that I have never in my puff seen a grown man so dumb-struck and then so unbelievably happy. 'Erimem? My Pharaoh?'

Erimem fairly skipped the steps to him and took his hands. 'Hello, Antranak. My dear friend.'

He looked at her hands and then he smiled so widely I thought he'd turn into a human Pez dispenser and the top of his head would flip off. 'I don't believe it.' A sudden realisation seemed to hit him. He remembered just exactly what rank Erimem held – or at least had held – and he really did drop to his knees. 'Oh, my Pharaoh.'

Erimem tugged on his hands firmly. 'Stand up, old friend. You do not have to kneel to me.'

'I cannot.' The soldier shook head head and stared at the stone floor. 'You are a god. I saw you leave. I saw you go...'

'...to the stars,' Erimem finished for him. She pulled at his hands but he still resisted.

'And you have returned. You have been gone for so long.' Jesus, he adored her. Not in a creepy way or anything. This was almost like family. 'My Pharaoh Erimem. You have come back to us.'

'For a short visit,' Erimem said firmly. 'Only for a short visit to see my friend. My mentor. My Antranak.' She pulled at his hands again and he finally pushed himself upright. She looked at his for a moment then tapped his stomach, which showed signs of starting to swell. 'You are prospering.'

Antranak considered feigning outrage but couldn't find it in him. 'The new Pharaoh is, rather unfortunately, a skilled diplomat. I haven't had a good war in years.'

'My poor Antranak,' Erimem said with the kind of friendly sarcasm you only get away with when it's somebody who really loves you. 'You must be so bored.'

'I am,' Antranak chuckled. 'I fear I really am.'

Erimem's face became more serious. 'And Fayum?' she asked. 'Is he a good Pharaoh?'

'He is a fine Pharaoh,' Antranak assured her. 'But he is not you,' he added quietly.

That made Erimem smile and I worked out what their relationship was. A favourite uncle with his favourite niece.

For the first time Antranak looked away from Erimem and his eyes stopped on Adam. I think he must have sensed this was someone else who was in her affections. 'And this?'

Erimem glanced at Adam. 'He is with me,' she said firmly.

'A bodyguard?' asked Antranak.

'No,' she answered meaningfully. 'He is *with* me.' No doubting what she meant there.

Antranak gave Adam an appraising sort of look, weighing up if he was good enough for Erimem, and deciding pretty quickly that *nobody* was good enough for her. 'Oh. Is he a god also?'

'I'm Scottish, that's pretty close.' Adam answered. He was annoyed at being talked about while still standing there.

Antranak ignored the interruption. 'Does he have a name?' he asked Erimem.

Adam answered. Yeah, he was pretty pissed off. 'Yes. He also has ears and a tongue in his head. I'm Adam. Adam Docherty.'

Erimem got between the two men and spoke quietly to Adam. 'Normally if someone spoke like that to the mighty Antranak they would not keep a tongue in their head for long.' She turned to the soldier. 'Antranak, I would prefer that he did not lose his tongue.'

'Don't ask why.' Okay. That slipped out without me thinking. I apologise for the smut.

Antranak looked at the rest of us. 'More?'

'I rarely travel alone,' Erimem said. She gave my arm a squeeze before introducing us all. 'This is Andy. Ibrahim is a descendant of my brother, Mentu, from far in the future. With him is his wife Helena.'

'From not so far in the future.' Yeah. That came out without me thinking as well.

Helena wrinkled her nose at me. 'Cheeky mare.'

There was something starting to cloud Antranak's face. Not

106

suspicion... trepidation maybe. 'Why have you returned?' he asked Erimem. 'Is Egypt in danger? Are you here to take the throne from Pharaoh?'

Her eyebrows lifted at the last question. 'Should I?'

'I am always loyal to my Pharaoh,' Antranak answered – without actually answering.

'Where is Fayum?' Erimem asked gently.

'He is...' Antranak faltered. 'I mean Pharaoh is at an act of diplomacy.'

Erimem's head tilted in confusion. 'You sound disapproving.'

'An act of *diplomacy* with his new wife,' Antranak explained. 'He sealed peace with one of the tribes to the East by marrying one of their princesses earlier today.'

Understanding dawned and Erimem smirked. 'So his diplomacy is...'

'The kind he enjoys,' Antranak said sourly.

I do think Antranak might have preferred a big punch up but this Pharaoh Fayum's way sounded pretty groovy to me. 'Make love, not war. A hippy Pharaoh.'

'Or just a horny one,' Ibrahim added.

Antranak scowled suspiciously. 'What is this "horny" you speak of?'

'Virile,' Helena explained quickly. 'Virile and manly.'

That seemed to soothe Antranak. 'Ah, it is a compliment. Good.'

Erimem finally answered one of the soldier's questions. 'No, I am not here to take the throne back, Antranak. That is not my life now.'

That appeased Antranak as well. He may grumble about Pharaoh Shagger the First but I got the feeling he was spectacularly fond of his king and brutally loyal to him. 'I doubt if I can imagine the life you live among the gods.'

'I am not with the gods,' Erimem explained. 'I... travel.'

'Travel where?' Antrtanak frowned.

Erimem just wafted a hand upwards. 'To the stars. To distant places.'

And I acted like a tit again. 'To explore strange new worlds. To seek out new life and new civilizations. To boldly go where no one has gone before.'

Erimem sighed and gave me a look. 'Is there a reason we are friends?'

'I'm adorable?'

'Don't worry,' Ibrahim said to Antranak. 'They're always like this. Gods help us.'

A smile returned to Antranak's face. 'It pleases me to see my Pharaoh so at ease with so many.'

Erimem returned the smile. 'I have grown up.'

'You have,' Antranak nodded with a near paternal pride before he scowled again. 'But did you have to grow hair? It looks... uncivilised.'

'It is often very cold where I live, my friend,' Erimem laughed. 'Even the mighty Antranak would grow his hair to deal with London in winter.'

'Lon-don?' Antranak grunted. 'I've nver heard of it.'

Erimem's lips pursed thoughtfully. 'It is a very strange place, but I like it.' She allowed herself a moment of just looking at her old mentor before she became all business again. 'But now I must tell you of the reason I am here.'

'Yes?'

'I am on a quest,' Erimem told Antranak. 'A quest to find the Rings of Maat.'

'Why?' Antranak asked. 'What is this quest?'

'To save the world,' Erimem answered honestly. 'These rings will placate a great evil more than three thousand years from now and they will save the entire world from destruction.'

It sounded like bollocks mumbo-jumbo to me but Erimem knew her audience, and Antranak believed her without a second thought. 'Very well, my Pharaoh. I will help in any way I can, but I fear that your quest is already a lost cause. These rings disappeared some years ago when you were perhaps fourteen or fifteen summers old.'

Adam leaned forward with interest. 'Did you find out what happened to them?'

Antranak looked disappointed. 'If I had they would be here. No,' he conceded, 'I never found them or any clue of who stole them.'

Erimem wasn't giving up. 'Do you know exactly when this

happened? Which day?'

'I would have the records in my rooms.'

Erimem had already come to her decision. 'Then I would ask you to find that exact day and tell it to me.'

Antranak was a screamer. Who knew?

Mind you, first trip through time was weird for us all. Most of us threw up after our first journey... and that's exactly what Antranak did. All over the floor of the time travel chamber in Erimem's villa. A little robot trundled out to disintegrate the up-chuck. Rather than explain robots we took Antranak out onto the terrace of the villa to get a bit of fresh air. We didn't explain that the Woolly Mammoths in the villa's grounds were living holograms. Nope. Not even going close to that.

'This is where you live?' Antranak asked. 'This is the future?'

'More or less,' Erimem answered evasively. Her habitat existing in its own little artificial side universe was not something I was going to explain either. Nope. A bit of good old fibbing was the answer.

I handed a glass of water to Antranak. He looked at the clarity of the glass and then drank the liquid. 'Thank you. I appreciate it being cold.'

Erimem dropped a hand onto her friend's shoulder. 'If it is any consolation, the great warrior Antranak was not the first to react that way on his first journey through time.'

'No?' He didn't sound convinced.

'You did better than most,' I fibbed. 'The majority of people react a lot worse than you did.'

'Thank you.' He looked a bit relieved by that.

'Your body will adapt,' Erimem continued.

He frowned uncertainly. 'Are you sure?'

She gave him the smile she saved for special friends. 'Do you see any of us being sick?'

'No.'

'You get used to it,' I confirmed. 'You hardly notice it after a while.'

'I am not a god,' Antranak said uncertainly. 'Your ways are

not mine.'

'You *will* get used to it,' Erimem promised. 'Have I ever lied to you?'

Antranak frowned at her. That expression was enough to tell you how close they were. 'We both know the answer to that is "yes", don't we?' His face relaxed into a smile and she returned it.

'Well, since I became Pharaoh, then?' Erimem hedged. 'Have a misled you since then?'

'No,' he conceded. 'You have not.'

A baby mammoth ambled over in search of some attention and Erimem rubbed the top of its head affectionately. It let her pamper it until a parp from its mother sent it running back to her side.

'I have never seen such a beast,' Antranak said. 'Is it... I don't know how to find the words for my question. Is it *new*?'

'Old,' Erimem answered. 'They are a very old species, but Andy brought these here for me.'

Antranak looked at me. He was working out if I was a god, too. I think he was getting close to his saturation point for weird.

'Maybe we should move on?' I suggested. Erimem agreed and we headed back inside. Adam was watching football on the huge TV.

'You couldn't forget about football for a day?' I asked.

He didn't look back. 'It's Arsenal.'

Ah, well. That was different. 'What's the score?'

'Moving art?' Antranak sounded bewildered.

'Not exactly,' Erimem answered. 'It is a way of seeing what is happening in another place. It is a very clever trick.'

'A trick?' That seemed to appease Antranak. It was a description he could understand. 'Like a soothsayer's vision.'

'Something like that,' Erimem agreed.

I switched the TV off. 'It's not the same without a crowd,' I grumbled.'

Adam wasn't convinced about my excuse for switching off. 'Or when your lot ship a goal.'

I resisted the temptation to stick my tongue out at him. *Just.*'I could still persuade Erimem to dump you, you know.'

Neah. He didn't believe that any more than I did. 'You'll

equalise before long. Their keeper is rank.'

'He's more scared of crosses than Dracula,' I muttered, hoping see a long ball challenging the keeper.

Antranak was completely bemused. 'It's a different language,' he said to Erimem. 'Do you understand what they are saying?'

Erimem's nose wrinkled. 'Some of it.' She leaned closer to Antranak. 'Between you and I, I actually really don't care.'

Adam gave me a look. I gave him exactly the same one back. 'I say we both dump her for that,' I said.

He nodded.

Boom! That was it. That was the moment Adam and I both knew we were cool and accepted where we stood in Erimem's lives. Best mate and boyfriend, accepting each other. And we could even talk football without any bile. He supported Hearts. Different league – in a different country – so we couldn't fall out over that. Good guy.

Erimem had put her business head on again. 'We should go.'

Antranak didn't like the sound of that. Poor bloke. 'To travel again?' I quite liked him. He was totally out of his depth but ready to do whatever Erimem asked.

'Don't worry,' I said, nudging Antranak. 'I'll bring water.'

'Thank you.'

We were back in Pharaoh's Palace and it looked the same – only different. Trees weren't quite as tall, different flowers were in bloom, giving the place a completely different scent and the heat wasn't quite so oppressive. It was a more temperate time of year. There was a different feeling in the Palace's grounds, too. We'd seen soldiers when we were there a few years later but here the place was full of them. We were all aware of it, including Antranak.

Ibrahim was the one who commented on. 'Are we in the middle of a military action?'

Antranak shook his head. 'This is a different palace, a different Pharaoh.' He measured his words so that he didn't insult either Pharaoh. 'The Pharaoh of this time… your mighty father,' he added to Erimem, 'secured the peace, as did you, which my current Pharaoh now reinforces with diplomacy, but the foundations of it often came with war.'

'It is true,' Erimem said. 'My father was often away on great campaigns.'

'And you fought alongside him in his last,' Antranak added. Yeah, he was proud of that.'

'Only because you had me trained so well.' She sounded proud of that.

Antranak snorted. 'I agreed to have trained after you started training with my men without my consent. If I hadn't given my permission I would have to have had them put to death.'

Two passing soldiers emerged around the side of a building and snapped upright at the sight of Antranak.

'On your way,' Antranak barked.

The soldiers hustled on. Erimem waited till they were out of earshot before turning to Antranak. 'You enjoyed that.'

'Shouting at my men? Of course I did. They'd think there was something wrong if I didn't shout at them.' He sniffed. 'Besides, I remember those two. They deserve to be shouted at.'

I started towards the Temple of Maat but Erimem caught my arm. 'We were caught last time because too many of us went inside. It would be easier if Antranak and I went into the temple.'

'And what do we do?' Adam asked. 'Stand about like spare pricks at a wedding?'

That was phrase which meant nothing to Erimem. She looked back blankly.

'He just wants to know what you want us to do.' I translated.

Erimem pointed to a narrow gap between two large bushes. 'There is a garden of contemplation there.' A little gleam appeared in her eyes. 'Go there and pray upon your sins – which I know are many.'

'And a lot of fun,' I answered.

Erimem turned and walked towards the temple. Antranak dropped into step at her shoulder, half a pace behind. He glanced back at us. 'Try not to get caught.'

He was feeling a bit more confident now he was back in his own patch. I suppose it helped that he was with a living god.

We sneaked into that little garden Erimem had mentioned and you know something? It was gorgeous. Thick, luxurious grass, various flower bushes at the side of really ornately carved stone benches. The bizarre – and quite brilliant – thing was that the thick bushes were somehow arranged so that they appeared thick and lush on the outside but from the inside it was possible to see the dark shapes of people passing by.

'I don't like this,' Adam muttered.

'Neither do I.' Ibrahim was peering through the hedge, trying to pick out the details of the Palace. 'All that history out there and we're stuck in here, skulking like naughty kids.'

'Better here than in some dungeon,' Adam said.

I had to agree with that. But I agreed with Ibrahim more. We'd never hidden away when we went on our travels before. I suppose this was different. This was Erimem's own patch. I just wasn't sure I wanted to hide out when I'd learn more about her by seeing the world she grew up in. I was going to suggest we just sneak out for a five minute look around when we all heard footsteps running closer. They were small and light, not the heavy clomp of soldiers. A few seconds later and attractive girl somewhere between sixteen and twenty ran into this little garden. She was shocked to see somebody already there.

Also shocked was the man in his teens who ran in after her. He was somebody important. He wore gold rings and bands around his biceps, as well as an ornate gold pectoral. His eye make-up was a mixture of lapis lazuli blue and gold. The most striking thing was the confident way he moved. He was playful and boyish and had a randy goat gleam in his eye.

They both screeched to a stop when they saw us waiting in the little garden. The girl looked slightly embarrassed. The man, not so much.

'What are you doing here?' he asked.

The words were out of my mouth before I could stop them. 'Not what you were thinking about doing here, that's for sure.'

Okay. I thought that was going to get us into real trouble. The man's eyes widened in surprise at being spoken to like that but then he broke into a huge smile.

'You have no idea who I am, do you?'

My stomach lurched. He really *was* somebody important.

Ibrahim knew what to say. 'We do not, my Lord, but we are visitors to the Palace, preparing to give thanks at the Temple of

Maat. We do not even live in Thebes. If we have caused offence, I apologise.'

This young man waved the words away. 'There is no need to apologise. It's rather liberating not to be recognised.' The smile broadened. 'Though if my father arrives, I would advise you to recognise him and prostrate yourselves. He will be easy to spot. We will be the one everybody is calling Pharaoh.'

My stomach dropped.

So did Ibrahim's. 'Pharaoh? So you're...'

The young lad's smile got even broader. 'Yes.'

'Oh, god,' Ibrahim groaned.

That just made the lad laugh. 'No, that's my father.'

An almost familiar voice came from a shadow passing outside of the garden. 'Mentu!'

'And that's my sister,' the prince said.

Adam's eyes widened. 'That's...'

'Erimem,' the prince supplied.

Erimem's approach seemed to terrify the prince's randy young lady friend. 'Please don't let her catch me here,' she begged.

He was more relaxed about being found. 'You've done nothing to be ashamed of.' He sounded a bit disappointed about that.

'She will not see it that way,' the girl said desperately. 'I am her handmaid not yours.'

'I am not afraid of my sister,' Mentu said firmly before shrugging in confession. 'All right, I am a little afraid of her, but she won't say anything to you, Hanek.'

'Hanek?' the word tumbled from Ibrahim's mouth.

'What of it?' the prince demanded suspiciously. Ibrahim didn't see that suspicion, though. His mind was doing cartwheels. 'Then you are Prince Mentu?'

'Yes.'

Ibrahim just beamed at him. 'Then it is really a huge honour to meet you. To meet you both. A real honour.'

'I'm sure it is.' Mentu had the look of somebody who was used to being told that.

Helena could see that Ibrahim was in need of reigning himself in. She caught his hand. 'Ibrahim?'

'It's fine,' Ibrahim said happily. 'In fact it's great.'

The younger Erimem's voice came from outside again. 'Mentu.'

Mentu touched Hanek's arm gently. Actually, I'd say *tenderly*. He had genuine affection for the girl – as well as filthy intentions. 'I will go and deal with my sister.'

Hanek pointed at the back of the garden. 'I will leave through the gap.'

Mentu's face had gone completely serious. 'None of you will repeat anything of this,' he told us.

'Absolutely,' Ibrahim agreed, 'nut can I say again, it was a real honour to meet you?'

'Of course,' Mentu said, but he wasn't really paying us any attention now. 'I'll go and deal with Erimem,' he told Hanek. With that, he headed out of the garden, leaving the girl behind.

'It was an honour meeting you as well,' Ibrahim said to her.

She just looked at him blankly for a second then smiled. 'Thank you,' she said and then scooted off to the back of the garden and eased through a gap none of us could actually see was there. I suppose that was its point. There's no use in having a secret exit/entrance that everybody can see.

'What's got into you?' I asked Ibrahim. 'You weren't even that star-struck when you met Elvis or George Best.'

Ibrahim was damn near bouncing with excitement. 'That was him. Mentu. Erimem's brother.' It started to dawn on a few of us but there were still a few blank faces. 'That was my great, great however many times grandfather.'

Adam picked up the gist. 'And she was…'

Ibrahim nodded. He was just so happy. 'My all-those-greats grandmother.' He sank down on the bench. He was close to tears, he was so happy. 'Oh, god. I never thought I could meet them.'

'And you just blocked them,' I said. Yeah, I was not in good form with controlling my gob on this trip.

Ibrahim frowned. 'What?'

'They weren't coming in here to hold hands,' Helena explained tactfully.

Adam had less tact. 'There was at least snogging planned.'

'Possibly even some getting jiggy,' I added. Well, I started the hassle, I should hit the *coup de grace*.

'Ohhhh.' Ibrahim looked startled and then a bit mortified. 'They were going to…'

'Alfresco?' Helena said quietly. 'Now I know where you get that from.'

And Ibrahim looked mortified again. Or perhaps we should just call him Ibrahim the Cock-Blocker from now on. Or does that sound a bit too Viking?

It was info I didn't need to know anyway and I said so. 'TMI.'

Adam's voice changed the subject, for which at least two of us were enormously grateful. 'There she is.'

'What?' Ibrahim asked.

'Erimem. There.'

We hurried over and joined Adam by the entrance. We all sort of peered through the hedge. It was Erimem all right, but she was so young. At a guess I'd say she was fifteen or sixteen. Maybe a year less, maybe a year more. It was kind of hard to gauge because, well, she was pretty much bald. There was just the same little brush of stubble darkening her head as her brother. She and Mentu were chatting about five metres away and we just shamelessly eavesdropped.

'I have been looking for you,' she said. She sounded younger, not as confident as the version we were travelling with, but she was talking to Mentu the way only sisters speak to brothers.

'And now you have found me.' Yep, and he was talking in the bloody annoying way only brothers speak to sisters.

'What are you doing here?' she asked.

'Can I not seek spiritual comfort?' he answered haughtily.

She wasn't buying the act. 'You would seek comfort with the temple girls.'

Out came the fake outrage. 'You make that sound dishonourable.' He sniffed slyly. 'And I know you have visited them yourself.'

Wooooah, Nellie! Now *that* was something we'd be discussing later.

She batted the accusation away. 'It is expected for me to visit the temple.'

'I believe you,' he said in an arch tone that said he wasn't buying a word. And then he changed the subject. The sod. 'Why were you looking for me?'

'Because our father is looking for you,' Erimem explained with a sigh, 'and I wanted to warn you.'

Mentu's playful mood evaporated more than a little. It was clear that being summoned by their father usually meant bad news. 'What is it about?'

'I don't know,' she answered, 'but you should be doing something he would approve of when his men find you.'

'He doesn't care what I do,' Mentu said sourly. 'Thutmose is his heir. He's the one that matters.'

Erimem had obviously taken note of the hurt in her brother's voice and spoke soothingly to him. 'But you are still his son.'

'And you are his only daughter,' Mentu countered.

'Which means he doesn't notice me,' young Erimem answered, and there was a hint of bitterness in that side of the conversation, too. She had only ever talked about her father with absolute love and respect. I wondered if time was giving her rose-tinted specs when she thought about that relationship.

Mentu hadn't noticed anything in her tone. 'Which means you get away with doing whatever you want.'

'You sound jealous,' Erimem said lightly, but there was some challenge in there too. Even as a kid she wasn't one for backing down.

'Of course I am,' Mentu answered quickly, 'but I'm happy for your sake.' He changed tack again. 'Where were you going? After you found me, I mean.'

'Oh, nowhere.' Well, that was a lie and everybody who heard her speaking knew it. God, she was a terrible liar as a kid.

Mentu started to look smug again. 'That nowhere wouldn't involve training with Antranak's guards again, would it?'

'I don't...' she started to protest automatically, then stopped and scowled at him with a fury that might have burned him all the way through to the bone. 'How do you know?'

Mentu seemed offended that she had even asked. 'I may be a useless son and a terrible prince but I know things that happen in this palace.'

Erimem thought for a moment. 'If you were training with Antranak's guards our father would like that.'

Mentu was surprised by the suggestion. 'You don't mind giving up your time with them?'

Erimem wafted away his concern. 'I am better than you with every weapon already, and I will train when you go to see Pharaoh.'

That made Mentu chuckle. It was a nice sound, relaxed and more at ease. 'You have it all planned.'

'Of course.'

Mentu gave her arm a squeeze. 'Thank you. For warning me – and for sharing this training.'

'You are a terrible brother,' she said in a pantomime long-suffering way, 'but you are *my* terrible brother.'

'And you are my favourite sister,' he replied in an equally arch tone.

'I am your *only* sister,' she answered sharply.

'That's not my fault.'

They were bickering but they were laughing because it was all good fun. That's family.

'Come with me.' She nudged his arm. 'I will tell the guards not to hurt you too much.'

They started walking away along the path, trees and bushes occasionally taking then out of view. The bickered and laughed as they went.

'Jesus,' Adam breathed, 'she absolutely adores him.'

Helena nodded. 'He feels exactly the same way about her.'

It was something she had mentioned but seeing it... that was different. 'I know she talked about how much it hurt her when he died. I get it now. They were really close.'

Adam was fascinated by the receding figures. 'Look at them. They're mates as well as brother and sister.'

I nodded. 'He's older but she's looking out for him.'

'Ibrahim, are you all right?' Helena sounded more surprised than concerned.

Ibrahim was wiping tears out of his eyes with the heels of his hands. 'I don't think I am. They're my family. Distant but, not really because I met them. And I know what happens. I know none of them get to be together.' He pushed the heels of his hands into his eyes again. 'It's stupid. This is ancient history but it's family. Only family can get to you this way.'

Helena had just caught Ibrahim in a tight hug when Adam spoke. 'Somebody's coming.'

He was right. There were footsteps approaching.

'Look like you're praying,' Helena hissed.

I had no idea how ancient Egyptians prayed. 'How?'

Helena dropped to her knees and bowed her head towards the temple. 'Just do it.'

We had no idea if we were doing the right thing but we knew that if the worst happened we could easily zip off back to Erimem's Habitat in no time at all.

The footsteps got closer until they entered the little garden. We kept our eyes down. No need to act suspiciously or...

'What a devout, penitent group of friends you have, Pharaoh,' Antranak said. 'So deep in their prayer.'

'Very pious, aren't they?' Erimem agreed. 'So unlike my friends normally.'

We scrambled to our feet and I gave Erimem a full-on scowl. 'It's you.'

'Obviously,' she smirked.

'Yeah, but *you* you,' I answered. 'Not you with the bald head.'

She didn't follow me and said as much. 'What are you talking about?'

'We saw you,' I explained. 'The you from this time. Young little cute you with the baldy head.'

'I liked the bald head,' Antranak offered. 'Far more civilised.'

Erimem wasn't listening to Antranak, just this once. She was fascinated by the thought of seeing her younger self. 'Where was I?'

Adam and I pointed at exactly the same time but I got the words out first. 'You went that way.'

Ibrahim caught her hand. 'You weren't alone. Erimem,' he said. 'I saw him.'

A frown wrinkled her brow. 'Him?'

'Mentu,' Ibrahim answered simply. 'We met Mentu.'

The effect was incredible. She turned and headed back for the way out. 'Where is he?' She was desperate to see him again.

'He left with you,' Adam said. 'You were warning him that your father looking for him.'

You could actually see the memories coming back to her.

They lived in her eyes and her expression. 'I remember this day,' she said softly. 'My father was so pleased when Mentu was found learning the arts of war.'

'Because you warned him,' I said.

She didn't really hear me. She was in her own thoughts now. 'Mentu. My dear Mentu. Thutmose was always with my father and Teti... poor Teti had to be cared for. I think too many of his ancestors came from the same families.'

She had something to say so I tried to help her say it. 'That left you and Mentu.'

'We were great friends,' she said, love poured out in every word, 'even if he did treat my handmaidens as a buffet for his sexual shenanigans.'

'Good word,' I said.

'We saw Hanek as well,' Ibrahim added.

That made Antranak frown. 'Hanek? I know that name.' He found the answer somewhere in his memory. 'Oh, yes. One of your handmaidens. She ran away...'

Erimem shook her head. 'I let her go,' she corrected the soldier. 'She was accused of a crime she did not commit and she was carrying Mentu's child. The beginning of a line that would lead to Ibrahim.' She looked at Ibrahim with so much affection. 'My nephew.'

'Auntie.' Ibrahim said the word as if it just strange saying it to her. Strange but right. At least for this moment. 'I met them,' he said quietly. I met them.'

'And he was a bit of a lad, your brother,' Helena pointed out.

Erimem frowned, wondering if some criticism of her brother was coming. 'What do you mean?'

Helen's eyebrows lifted in amusement. 'He certainly checked out my cleavage..

That broke the tension. Pretty much everybody laughed.

'And he couldn't keep his eyes off mine,' I agreed, even though he'd only had a bit of a look.

A smile pushed itself onto Erimem's face. 'I should not laugh. I shouldn't.'

'But you're going to,' Helena said.

Erimem nodded. 'It just sounds very much like Mentu,' she laughed. 'It is no excuse but things are different here.'

Helena waved the concerns away. 'If it levels things up at all, I checked out his arse. Like a peach.'

'Do you mind?' Ibrahim protested. 'That's my grandad.'

'Do you think I could see him?' Erimem asked softly.

Helena's smile became more fixed, less spontaneous. 'Well, you *could*.'

'You don't think I should?'

I understood Helena's concerns. 'What would you do? Warn him what was coming?'

'I could,' Erimem said urgently. 'It would…' she stopped as the truth hit her and it was horrible to see. 'It would destroy time, wouldn't it?'

'Yeah,' I said. 'It's shit, isn't it?'

'Yes, it is,' she agreed sadly. 'But if I warn him would I also warn Thutmose? Teti? Antranak? Would I warn myself? Time must not change.'

Adam's voice came from the way out. 'Erimem. Come here.'

'What is it?' She moved across to join him and followed his pointed finger. 'Look. There. If you look past the trees.'

She whispered the name. 'Mentu.'

We joined them at the exit. In the distance, Mentu nudged the younger Erimem. The girl nudged him back. He tried again. She replied in kind. Even at this distance we heard them laughing.

Erimem remembered that moment. She remembered exactly what had been going through her head at the time. A smile I couldn't read appeared on her face.

'I think we should go home,' she said.

'All right,' I agreed.

Adam was the only one still thinking about the task at hand. 'Did you get what you needed?'

'I thought so,' she answered, holding up a pair of ornate gold rings. 'Yes, I got more than I came for.'

'Come on,' I said. 'Let's go.'

We landed in Erimem's Habitat and things were very, very wrong.

The place was shaking. It was like there was an earthquake. But that was impossible. It wasn't on a planet. There wasn't any real Earth to quake under our feet.

We staggered, trying to stay on our feet. I tried to get to the controls to see WTF was happening.

That was when Adam yelped. 'Where's Erimem?'

He was right. She wasn't there. She hadn't come back with us. I ran through into the main lunge. Olivia was there, hanging to the door frame, Tom was sprawled on the floor. I wasn't too worried about him. I ran across to Olivia. 'Are you all right?'

She shook her head. 'What's happening?

'We don't know. Is Erimem here?'

Another shake of the head.

And the Habitat shook twice as hard.

There was a crackling sound from the travel room and we all stumbled back to the door. Erimem had just arrived. She looked worried. More than worried. Ashen.

Adam was at her side straight away. 'What is it? What happened?'

She shook off any support. She had her game face on. She was in Pharaoh mode not girlfriend. That switch was something Adam was going to have to get used to. 'Our task is not complete,' she said.

The villa shook again and Mammoths trumpeted in fear outside.

'What do we have to do?' Helena asked.

'I have done half of it,' Erimem said. 'My grandfather told me that the rings were on Cleopatra's body when she was found by the Roman soldiers, but she was not wearing them when she was prepared for burial.'

Adam thought like a copper. 'Somebody nicked them?'

Erimem nodded. 'They were stolen from her body.'

'Thieving bastards.' The words were out before I had time to think about them. 'So what's the job?'

Erimem turned and headed back into the travel room. 'I have already placed the rings on her corpse's fingers. They will be stolen soon. We are going to get them back.'

I like Alexandria. We've been there a few times. It's vibrant, lively, full of chatter and discussion and... and not this time it wasn't. There were Romans everywhere at every street corner. The locals were staying indoors and those doors were securely locked.

'Where is this place?' Antranak asked.

'Alexandria,' I answered.

He looked blankly at me. 'Never heard of it.'

'It is Egypt's capital,' Erimem said, ushering us towards a shadowy alley between two tall buildings.

Her answer took Antranak by surprise. 'The capital? What of Thebes?'

Erimem gave her old friend a sympathetic look. 'This is more than a thousand years after our time, my friend. Many things have changed.' She pointed at a large, tall building in the middle of a square. 'The last Queen of Egypt, the last Pharaoh for more than two thousand years took her own life in that building.'

'That's where Cleopatra committed suicide?' Adam asked, staring at the mausoleum. It was a huge, impressive place. She had made a statement with her death. 'Was it really suicide?' he pressed.

'Yes,' Erimem nodded, 'I was with her.'

That took Adam by surprise. 'Seriously?' I'd forgotten that this happened long before we met him.

'It was her only choice,' Erimem said. 'Had she lived she would have been taken back to Rome, stripped naked and marched through the streets before being executed in public.'

The story had pushed Antranak into a fury. He looked set to take on the entire Roman army single handed. My money wuld have been on him to win, too. That was the kind of burning anger he had. 'Who is this Rome? I would kill them to their last descendant for harming a Pharaoh.'

Erimem put a calming hand on her old friend's arm. 'Be calm, Antranak. This war was lost long after our time, and long before the time in which I now live. It is part of history.'

Antranak just shook his head. 'I do not understand.'

She squeezed his arm again. 'Trust me, my old friend. Just trust me.'

An exasperated sigh escaped that bear of a man. 'Of course I trust you, my Pharaoh, but I do not understand this world.'

'There.' That was Olivia. We had all come back to

Alexandria. The reckoning was that if anything went irreparably wrong, at least we'd all be together in the one time zone. It was good that she was there, not just because I wanted to know she was safe, but because she was the one who hadn't been distracted from the mausoleum. She had spotted a group of around ten or a dozen Romans slipping out of the mausoleum, putting pouches into their belts.

'Roman troops,' Helena said, 'and they're pocketing whatever they've stolen.'

Adam got straight to the point. 'Okay, what's the plan?'

'We are going to steal it back,' said firmly.

'Light fingered burglary?' I suggested hopefully. 'Something sneaky and subtle?'

Erimem just gave me a look. 'No.'

'Didn't think so somehow.'

We followed the Romans through the streets of Alexandria until they reached a quiet passage that was in shadow. There was nobody else there and we all instinctively knew that was where it would happen.

'You have stolen from the dead,' Erimem called after the Romans.

The Romans kept moving. We moved after them faster.

'You have stolen from the dead,' Erimem called again.

This time the Romans stopped and turned. The one who seemed to be their leader looked back at us with contempt. 'What did you say?'

'If you are too old to hear or too stupid to understand, I will say it again,' Erimem said carefully. 'You have stolen from the dead, and you have stolen from Egypt.'

The Romans reached for the hilts of their short gladius swords' 'Get out of our way or you will join her.'

Antranak had been waiting for an excuse to erupt and that was it. 'You threaten my Pharaoh?' He sounded like thunder.

The Roman looked confused. 'What Pharaoh?'

Erimem answered very calmly. It's when she's cold-calm like that… that's when you know the shit's going down and she is really up for it. 'Put down what you stole and I will let you leave,' she said.

The Romans didn't quite believe what they'd heard. They laughed. 'We are soldiers of Rome,' one of them said.

'And we don't care.' Well, that was out of my gob before I knew I was going to say it.

'Return what you stole,' Erimem repeated. 'Give it to us now. I will not ask again.' She meant it.

The Roman leader didn't heed the warning. 'Not with no tongue in your head.'

He put his hand on his sword, and that was when every kind of shit cut loose. There were ten of them and less of us. It didn't matter. We took them by surprise or some damn thing. That first soldier only manage to get his sword half way out of the scabbard before Antranak's own sword slashed down across the soldier's wrist slicing the hand off. The sword slid back into the scabbard. The Roman just stared at the stump. Antranak was already moving at the next soldier. He was a big man but he moved fast. That huge sword of his hacked down another Roman. Erimem was on the move as well, those khopesh daggers slicing the arms of another Romans. The next in line had drawn his sword. A blur from the side slammed into him and smashed him into the wall. He dropped like a stone. Adam made sure the man he'd attacked was out cold and swept up his sword. That was the cue for the rest of us to pile in. Fists, swords, daggers... Olivia had brought her cutlass and was showing why they're called her the *Scarlet Queen*. Ibrahim twatted one soldier with a piece of wood he'd found while Helena caught another by the wrist, twisted and flipped him onto his back. Somehow she was holding his sword by the time he landed.

Antranak and Erimem were having a ball, driving two of the others backwards. She used speed and mobility and he had brute power and an amazing amount of skill in his use of that big sword. He looked disappointed when the soldier he was fighting dropped a leather purse and ran.

'Coward,' he bellowed.

Erimem's opponent realised he was the last man standing and threw a heavy pouch at her, then turned and legged it after his mate.

'This one is also a coward,' Erimem said with satisfaction.

She passed me the leather pouch she had caught then scooped up the purse Antranak's victim had thrown. 'Search for the rings. They are all we need to find. Nothing else.'

The Romans had all helped themselves to various trinkets. Thieving bastards. I put the sandal to the groin of the nearest one because they deserved it.

Stupid movie. It really hurt.

Sandals are crap for kicking guys in the nuts.

'Is this them?' Adam had plucked two rings from a leather purse and held them out to Erimem.

She took the rings and gave them a quick look. 'Yes.' She slid the rings into a pouch. 'Now we can go. You remember how this works?' she said to Antranak.

A little bit of amused exasperation appeared on Antranak's face. 'My Pharaoh, I am not quite so useless as...' his voice faded and his eyes widened in surprise. Behind him a Roman leader shambled to his feet and started to run, a bloodied dagger in his hand. Antranak staggered and clutched at the wall. He put a hand to his back and it came away slick and crimson. The sight of his own blood acted like an adrenalin rush and he pushed himself away from the wall, ready to give chase but the Roman was already long gone.

Erimem caught one arm to keep him upright while Helena was already by his side, tearing at his uniform so she could see the wound.

'We need to get him back home,' Helena said urgently. 'Now.'

'How bad is it?' Antranak gasped. He caught sight of the blood smeared on his hand. 'The blood is dark. That is not a good sign.'

'Are you a doctor?' Helena snapped.

'She asks if you are a healer,' Erimem translated.

'No,' Antranak gasped.

Helena tore a piece of her dress free and pressed it against Antranak's side. 'Well, I am, so leave the diagnosis to me.'

That bewildered him further. 'A woman?'

'Nothing wrong with your eyesight anyway,' Helena said briskly. 'We need to get him home *now*.'

We reached for our time travel rings.

Back in Erimem's Habitat, Antranak was face down on the couch. Helena had managed to staunch the flow of blood but the big man was pale.

'He needs to be in theatre,' Helena explained swiftly. 'I can't see the internal damage and I can't stitch him up until I know what it's like in there.'

Adam nodded. 'So we need to get him to a hospital?'

'And how do we explain an Egyptian general from way back?' Ibrahim asked.

'We don't,' Adam said quickly. 'I'm a copper so, if I found him being attacked... I take him to hospital.'

Helena agreed. 'And if I'm with you, we should be able to brush past the worst of the questions.'

'I will come with you,' Erimem said.

'And if I say no?' Adam asked.

'I will come anyway.'

Helena didn't try to argue. 'Okay, Andy, I'll tell you where you need to put us down.'

So I did. There's an alley just opposite the hospital Helena works at. It's always quiet except for young couples trying to find a quiet place for a knee trembler. Their knees will have really trembled if they saw four people arrive out of nowhere.

I have to fill this from what Erimem told me.

They arrived in the alley. Thankfully there were no snogging couples in mid-fumble. According to Her Queenieness, big strong Adam pretty much carried Antranak to A&E by himself. I think it was a group effort. Antranak's a big unit.

They got him in to the hospital and Adam dealt with the police side of things. It was a stabbing so it had to be reported, I suppose. Helena knew the staff on duty and got Antranak through whatever x-rays and scans needed done before they wheeled him into surgery. She knew the surgeon so she got herself into the OR as well. It pays to know people, I suppose. The Roman's dagger had got Antranak in the kidney. I'm not a doctor but Helena said the wound was a bad one. They struggled to get his bleeding stopped and had to keep giving him transfusions. There were fiddly bits that needed repaired and every time they fixed one they found another. That dagger had been twisted while it was inside and it had done a lot of damage. After about five hours in surgery, Helena came out briefly and talked to Adam. She wanted him to just grab Erimem and hang onto her if the worst happened. Antranak started slipping, his blood pressure dropping dangerously.

But he is a stubborn goat and he wasn't ready to die and he wasn't ready to leave his Pharaoh. He rallied and settled. Finally the surgery was finished and he was wheeled away to recover.

Adam told me that Erimem gave Helena the tightest hug he'd ever seen. She really does see Antranak as her favourite uncle. Her father was, well, her father, but I think Antranak fulfilled more of the *Dad* role in her young life.

Helena came back to the Habitat once Antranak was settled. She had me get some clothes together for Erimem. I asked Olivia if she would head back to the house in Hollywood to run interference if anyone asked where Erimem was. It was also… shit, I'm going to sound like a real cow, but I wanted Tom out of the Habitat. He's the only one of us who doesn't know where the door to the Habitat is based. I wouldn't say I'm warming to him but I'm more tolerant of him, but Erimem isn't ready to share her front door's address yet. So I asked Olivia to take him back to Hollywood. After he'd seen Helena and was sure there was nothing he could do for Antranak, Ibrahim went back to Hollywood as well. He thought – and he was right – that neither Olivia or Tom knew the people at the studio well enough to really deal with them. I should have gone back, too, but I didn't want to leave Erimem. I know she had Adam there but you don't leave your best mate.

I went back to the hospital with Helena. Adam was playing a blinder. It didn't come easy to him, fibbing to his colleagues, but he tried sticking to fibs rather than whopper-sized lies. *Why was his girlfriend there?* Erimem had heard him speaking in an Egyptian language, she felt a connection because of that, she was possibly the only person in London who spoke that language, hell she was doing them a favour by staying there offering to help…

Antranak woke up the next day and freaked out. The lights,

the machines, the tubes... he was lucky that it was only Helena and Erimem who were in his room. They calmed him down – well, Erimem did – and they got him to relax. I think that bit was Helena upping his meds. She kept him too out of it to talk to the police and Erimem had taken his time travel ring. Without that to translate he just kept talking in old Egyptian, which was fine because Erimem understood and translated for the doctors. I think there was a bit of editing done on the fly. He was weak for a few days, and mostly stoned off his tits on morphine. He became more lucid after a while though and seemed to have accepted that Erimem had brought him to some kind of heaven. He was sure he was dead.

'If you were dead it wouldn't hurt so much,' was Helena's answer.

There was such a sense of wonder and relief on his face when Erimem told him that after a while he would be able to go back to Egypt and carry on arguing with Fayum.

'Does that mean I must leave you?' he asked.

That love and devotion really did verge on paternal but it had so many other layers as well, not of them sleazy or nasty. Just genuine love.

Erimem smiled. 'Not yet, my dear Antranak.'

'However, we are breaking you out of this place,' Helena said.

Adam nodded. 'The police – the guards from this time – want to talk with you later today.

Erimem tapped the ring she had put back on Antranak's finger. After we leave you wait to a count of fifty and then twist the ring and we will meet you in my home.'

We didn't stay at Erimem's place. We arrived there and headed straight back to the golden age of Hollywood. Rosa was happy to see us – though to her we had only been gone a few minutes.

Erimem introduced Antranak as her uncle. He was going to be staying to recover from surgery. That was all Rosa needed to hear. From there on, she looked after Antranak and made sure he was comfortable. During the day he sat in the garden and recuperated. At night he told war stories, which were enough to put hair on your chest. Antranak just sort of fitted in. It felt like he belonged. And he felt that he was blessed to see Erimem again. He took a liking to Adam. He liked the way our resident copper had thrown himself at a Roman soldier even though he was unarmed. There were a few times they were discussing moves for disarming opponents when Rosa spotted them and went bing-bong about Antranak pushing himself too hard. It didn't matter, though. Erimem's boys were bonding.

One more thing I'm pleased about. Antranak liked Olivia and me. He thought we were some kind of angels or gods or mystical creatures but he liked that we were Erimem's friends. He was glad that she had people around who loved her.

I'm glad we were around too. Erimem is an odd mixture. In battle she's as hard as nails but other times she's goofy and daft and a great pal who has a hug on standby if you need one. I found her under the trees in the garden not long after we all got back to Hollywood. I didn't have to ask why she was on her own. She had held everything in while Antranak had been in hospital. She needed to not be in control for a bit. So I hugged her. That's what best mates do.

Our rather fab director Lisa Stone also took a shine to Antranak. The Stones had come over for dinner just after the movie started filming. She was nervous but she was doing well. She had one problem – the scene with the soldiers from the ancient Egyptian army looked slow and clunky. The soldiers weren't moving as they should.

'They need trained,' Erimem said. There was real mischief in her eyes as she looked to her old mentor. 'Antranak could train them to be soldiers.'

And he did.

He got them for five days in our garden – Rosa wouldn't let him go anywhere further than that – and he shouted at them, marched them and drilled them like he was back in Thebes. The poor sods looked shell-shocked after their first day with him, but it worked. By the time they were on set and the fight was happening, they looked the part. They had sharp, drilled movements. The guy playing their leader looked every inch the general of the Egyptian army – because that's exactly what he was. His injury had healed well enough for Antranak to appear in the film.

Filming was smooth. We all got pulled in to appear in the scenes we knew we were in. May I say that I am a femme fatale in my oh-so sharp outfit? And Olivia? Gorgeous with that sharp 1940s redder than red lipstick and her hair pulled into a Veronica Lake cut.

It's crazy for us to appear in a crummy old low budget movie. But we do.

You know what else is crazy? The last scene in the movie was a big fight. There were fists and feet flying everywhere. We all got moments in the fight. Even Stone was in there throwing fake punches. Tom wasn't keen on being on screen but Ibrahim and Adam cajoled him into it. By the end of things I'm pretty sure he was arranging to meet one of the dancing girls at the wrap party. That was the most like himself he's been in ages. I'm not saying that's a good thing but it does show that being with people has broken his fug a bit.

Antranak was sitting watching it all by this point, his scenes long since completed. He was utterly bemused by this fake fighting, but enjoying it all the same. He complaining about being "treated like an infant" by Rosa but he was loving that too. He was relishing this strange heaven that his Pharaoh had brought him to. I don't think he really ever cottoned on that it was just the future. It was simply too different. The horseless carriages, the moving pictures and the sounds that came from nowhere… they had to be magic but his Pharaoh controlled them, so it was all fine.

Eventually, Antranak had to go back, though. He had recovered quickly. He had the constitution of an ox and he was almost his old self by the end of filming, only wincing now and then when he twisted. Helena told him to keep that to a minimum for a few weeks but otherwise he would heal as good as new.

I went back to Egypt with Erimem and Antranak. It was best that she wasn't on her own after saying goodbye to him. Adam had asked about going but we agreed it might be a thing that was better for me to do. So we arrived back in the Temple of Maat and I sloped off to a dark corner for a skulk while they said what needed saying.

'Oh, my Antranak. I wish I was not leaving you here.'

'I am home, Pharaoh,' the soldier said simply, 'and you can come here any time you wish.' Doubt crept into his voice. 'Can't you?'

'There are rules even I must follow, my friend,' she answered uncertainly. 'You saw what happened when some things changed. Even Pharaohs have rules they must obey. But I swear by all you taught me that I will try to visit again.'

That seemed to be good enough for the big man. 'Then I will pray that the rules allow you to return and if they do not… if they do not I will give praises for this time spent with you and your friends. I am pleased that in your new life you are surrounded by people who love you.'

That took her off guard. 'Love is a large word, my friend.'

'And your friends have large hearts,' Antranak replied. 'I think your Adam is ready to give you his.'

She hadn't anticipated that from him either. 'That is not something I expected,' she admitted. ''Either as a subject we would discuss or that I might find someone like him.'

'Obviously he is not deserving of you,' Antranak said with a smile, 'and I would never presume to advise a god, but I think you are well matched. You both have good hearts.' A look of realisation dawned on his face. 'That reminds me, I have to attend an execution this afternoon. He's having his heart cut out.'

And the moment was gone.

'I will not be doing that with Adam,' Erimem laughed. 'Probably.' She gripped his hands tightly. 'I am so very glad I was able to see you again, my dear Antranak.'

'When you left, I never thought I would see you again,' Antranak said. It was like openly admitting this kind of emotion was hard for him. 'You have given me a great gift.'

'It was a gift to me,' Erimem answered.

'I would only say…' the general's lips pursed thoughtfully, 'I still don't like you with hair. It's terribly uncivilised.'

She laughed. 'You get used to it.'

He nodded, satisfied. 'I will sleep more comfortably in my bed at night knowing that you are well.'

'I am more than well, and I am happy.'

'Then I am content.'

They were stringing it out, holding off from saying goodbye, but that decision was made for them. A young man's voice came from the entrance to the temple.

'Antranak? Antranak?'

'I know that voice,' Erimem said warmly.

'So do I,' Antranak sighed. 'He probably wants to get another wife.'

She allowed herself another chuckle before releasing his hands. 'I must go.'

'Must you? Don't you want to see him?'

Erimem looked towards the source of the newcomer's voice. 'Yes – but Egypt can only have one Pharaoh.'

'He would love to see you,' Antranak pressed gently.

'And I him,' Erimem admitted, 'but we must go.'

Antranak, as ever, accepted his Pharaoh's wisdom. 'As you wish.'

'You will always be with me, Antranak,' she promised, 'and perhaps, just perhaps, we shall meet again.'

He straightened and game what I took to be their version of a salute. 'You are always my Pharaoh.'

'Goodbye, my dear Antranak.'

'My Pharaoh.'

She twisted her travel ring and the blue lightning carried her away. I was about to do the same when a figure appeared in the entrance and I slid deeper into the shadows. He was in his late twenties, I guessed, a shaved head and white kilt type of outfit. He moved confidently enough and hurried to Antranak.

'Ah. There you are,' the newcomer said.

Antranak turned to greet him. 'Yes, my Pharaoh?'

'I've been looking for you,' the Pharaoh said.

'And it seems you have found me,' Antranak replied.

The Pharaoh looked at the soldier with genuine concern. 'Are you all right, old friend? You seem... distracted.'

Antranak sighed. 'I was just thinking of your predecessor.'

'Ah.' S warm smile flitted across the Pharaoh's face. He had been fond of Erimem too. 'She is with the gods.'

'She is happy,' Antranak said gently.

'You sound certain.'

'I am,' Antranak replied firmly. 'Now, how can I help my Pharaoh?'

'I have been thinking.'

'Oh dear,' Antranak grumbled, 'that is never good to hear.'

Pharaoh feigned outrage. 'I could have your head cut off for that.'

'And who would you give orders to in order to get that done?' Antranak asked.

'You.'

'And you think I'll slice my own head off?'

'Probably not,' the Pharaoh admitted with a little chuckle.

'Who would keep you out of trouble if I did?' Antranak demanded good-naturedly.

'I see your point.' He caught Antranak's elbow and started leading him towards the door. 'There is a tribe out to the east. I think we should form an alliance with them.'

Antranak's shoulders slumped and he sighed loudly. 'Oh, what's the poor girl's name this time?'

'I don't know what you mean,' Pharaoh protested.

'Yes you do.'

'Marriages are a useful way to cement alliances.'

'You'll ruin your back, you know,' Antranak said in warning.

'Will you help me investigate this alliance?'

'Of course I will,' Antranak conceded, 'but how many wives do you actually *need*?'

'This will be the last, I promise.' Pharaoh assured him.

'Good.'

'Well, for now at least...'

They disappeared out of the temple, side by side, bickering and enjoying the rhythm of their banter like old friends do. I recognised that. I was glad that Antranak had such a good relationship with Erimem's successor. He was less deferential with this Fayum than with Erimem. It was a more straightforward friendship and there's nothing wrong with that.

But something they had talked about just made things click into place in my head. I knew what I wanted.

Knowing what I wanted and making it happen were not exactly

easy to put together. London is a great city, right? London in 2020 is... look, can we just forget 2020 ever happened and enjoy a repeat of 2012 instead? Everything is difficult in 2020. Plus... we were finding reasons to be back in 1940 a lot. What we'd done with the script and the rings had caused some minor rewrites in time. For one thing, Erimem's IMDB page now had more than three entries on it. And now I had an IMDB as well. Though I was just a minor supporting player in Erimem's movies.

We had to buy houses, we had to get Olivia's forged credentials set up and settle her, plus we had to spend a lot of time in 1940, doing interviews, some publicity, getting Erimem out of being cast as a villain in a Tarzan movie when RKO tried to borrow her... plus we had to enjoy the premiere.

Now that was an interesting night.

STONE

How in the hell did I get to be a producer?

I'm an ex-cop, ex-seamus and now ex-security chief. The boss at Centurion appreciated my work with Jennings and Milt so much he gave me Milt's office and told me to keep the pictures moving. I was glad the office was on the third floor. When I jumped it would make sure was toast.

What do I know about movies?

Well, not much, but it turned out, neither did Milt.

I had his schedule and I had a bunch of writers, directors and contract players. And I knew what movies I liked to pay my dime to see. I knew what most folks liked to see. You know what I thought when I sat down at that desk? I thought we could do better. So we did. We kept producing the movies that made us steady money. The cop quicks, the B-westerns, the private eye flicks and the really dumb comedies nobody knows they laugh at, but folks lap them up anyway. You know what we didn't do? We didn't dos serials, like Flash Gordon or Buck Rogers or Tarzan or Zorro. Why the hell not? These things played for fifteen weeks and the next year they'd run another fifteen. And maybe the year after that. Sure they'd only be part of a show so we'd only get part of the money, but it was regular and serials could reuse the same sets and actors for those fifteen weeks. So I got us into serials. I got us into pictures that could become a series of pictures, too. We already had a couple of those, but we needed more because they made good money and the sets were mostly built anyway. Doing all this work I made a terrible discovery about myself. I'm a good producer. I'm good at organising things and getting things done. I don't mind making decisions even if I might be wrong sometimes.

Yeah, I'm a good producer.

Jeez, that's depressing.

One good thing, I could make sure Lisa got more movies to direct. Only one thing bothered me about that. She'd started looking at classic novels to make into movies and I was going to have to read the damn books to make a decision. But we are going to make some classy pictures based on books. God, I hope she doesn't want to do Dickens.

I want us ready to do war movies. Erimem and her buddies, they know stuff about the war. They seem pretty sure America will be in it by the end of next year. If we are, we need to make war pictures. If we're in the war, I can't be the one making the pictures. I'll need to be in uniform. I hope they're right, because Hitler's crazy. He needs stopped because he will turn his eyes to America. But I hope they're wrong, too, because I don't want to see the look in Lisa's face when I tell her I'm joining up.

We'll deal with that when it happens.

You know what the first success I produced was? *The Jewels of Cleopatra*. It went out as part of a double feature with a neat little western horror called *Silver Guns*. The western was supposed to be the A-picture but I swapped them. I had a feeling.

I decided to have a premiere for it. Not something we usually do for any picture and especially not for a cheap and cheesy follow-up to a throwaway adventure. But like I said, I had a feeling.

We took a nightclub, invited movie stars, singers and anybody else in the papers to come and see it then get drunk on our dime at a glitzy nightclub. And we told them the press would be there. Nobody in this town turns down a picture in the paper – unless it involves a dame who ain't their wife.

I got mixed memories of being in nightclubs with Erimem and her buddies. First time we were fighting for our lives against a horde of zombies and second time was a movie premiere that kinda turned into an engagement party for me and Lisa. I liked the second one better.

This time it was business to launch the movie. The

punching… that came kind of natural to proceedings.

Centurion is not a big studio and the boss does not okay big checks for anything. Especially his employees. "Cheap" is one of his favourite words. Well, getting this club wasn't cheap but I know some people, plus they were getting good publicity because I know some famous people and a few of them agreed to slum it at a Centurion shindig. We got some pretty good names in. We didn't get Clark Gable or Tyrone Power. We didn't even Humphrey Bogart or Fred Astaire. We did get Errol Flynn, though. I guess the free bar and dames were a magnet for him. Ginger Rogers had a new comedy coming so she had to be seen around town. Robert Taylor and Cary Grant were around so I guess they had something new coming, too. There were a few other big names I was looking forward to seeing again.

I wasn't looking forward to an evening in a tux. These collars choke me and I still look like a sack of potatoes. Lisa… she looked like a knockout. So did the ladies in Erimem's party. They arrived in style in limos. The best we could rent on the cheap. They all looked like stars. The photographers kind of pushed Ibrahim and Helena aside because they weren't stars and focused on Erimem and on Andy and Olivia too. Adam knew he wasn't part of this bit of the night so he gave Erimem a kiss on the cheek and make his way over to me.

'Trying to get a contract?' I asked him. 'You look pretty good on screen.'

He shook his head. 'I'd rather stick to arresting people. How's life behind a desk?'

'I'd rather stick to arresting people.' I waved a waiter across. 'Two Scotch on the rocks.'

'You're a good man,' Adam said. He turned back to the flashing lights and glamorous celebrities being photographed. 'How did two dumb cops like us wind up in this life?' he asked.

'Definitely dumb luck for me,' I answered.

He thought, then nodded. 'Same for me.' He looked at Erimem for a long moment. 'She is way too good for me.'

Yeah, I understood that. 'I feel the same about Lisa. What do you say we just don't tell them that and hope they don't notice?'

'Works for me,' he agreed.

There was a guy in a cheap suit trying to make believe it was an expensive suit. I didn't know who he was. I didn't recognise him from the movies anyway. He gave Adam this look like he was something that should be scraped off a shoe. 'Look buddy, nobody minds you stickin' it to the coloureds on the hush-hush, but showing out in public, that ain't decent.'

I was ready to have the ass-hole thrown out but Adam answered first.

'Listen, shit-for-brains,' he said, 'if you ever repeat anything like that again, I'll punch you really hard in the face a second time.'

The weasel frowned. 'What do ya mean a second time?'

Adam's fist exploded on the weasel's jaw, putting him down flat on his ass. Blood showed at his nose and his mouth.

'That's a decent right hand you got on you, mister,' a familiar voice drawled from my shoulder.

I recognised the big man. 'Hi, Duke.'

'He earned it.' Adam glared at the bleeding weasel then turned and recognised my friend. 'Holy shit, you're John Wayne.'

'I guess I am,' Duke agreed then he nodded at the weasel, who had just struggled back to his feet. 'What did he do to deserve it?'

'He insulted my girlfriend,' Adam answered.

Duke sipped at his bourbon. 'Can't argue with a man defending his girl. Who is she?'

Adam pointed. 'Over there. The gorgeous one. Erimem.'

'Yeah. He insulted her?'

Adam nodded. 'Yep.'

The weasel didn't see the second right hand coming and a second later he was back on his ass, clutching his jaw. 'She's a good friend of mine,' Duke told the ass-hole. He rubbed his knuckles and took another slug of bourbon.

The weasel got to his feet and ran.

Adam looked taken aback by that. 'She wasn't joking about that?'

Duke shook his head. 'Hell, no. Did she tell you about the fight in the nightclub?'

'No,' Adam answered.

Duke pointed to a table. 'Let's get a drink and I'll tell you.'

ADAM

So John Wayne is my new best friend. Dad would be so chuffed. Not that I can tell him, but he really would be chuffed.

Wayne wasn't what I expected. They say people get more right wing as they get older. Always thought that was shite myself. My old man gets a wee bit further left every year. Wayne was fun and he was funny. Dry humour, taking the piss out of himself and really fond of his friends. He wondered why I wasn't hack home in uniform. Stone dug me out of that, saying I was a cop in LA on a job. That seemed good enough. Wayne was interested in the war, and sure America would be attacked or involved somehow. He wanted to be in uniform, to dight. I knew that would never happen, but he was honest and sincere about wanting to. Time travel is a really fascinating thing. You learn that history and reality aren't always the same. I'd have expected to dislike John Wayne. I didn't. I enjoyed his company. I liked the respect he showed Erimem and everyone else. Respect that was never patronising.

This life I had fallen into, this woman who I'd fancied for years and I'd accidentally wound up dating... it was worth bending a few rules and laws for. If that makes me a hypocrite or a shit cop, then... so what? I can live with that. It's a damn weird life for an Edinburgh laddie who grew up dreaming of being *Oor Wullie*. If you don't know who that is... you're missing out.

It's a weird life but it's mine and I love it.

ANDY

It was a great premiere. We got to play at being movie stars. We were wearing the swankiest dresses, all the hair do's and make-up… it was proper Hollywood glamour, the stuff we never do at home. It was *fun*!

The best thing was being there with these people I love, and seeing all the friendships and the pairings. This trip had put a lot of things in place in my head

Losing my parents so close together hurt. A lot. The way in caused problems between me and my brother? That hurt, too.

I'd found this second family. I was scared that me getting serious with somebody or Erimem finding someone special, that would break us up as a group. I didn't want to lose this new family. This whole trip showed that wasn't going to happen. We weren't losing anyone from the gang. It was just getting bigger.

So I relaxed and had a ball at the premiere.

'I want to get married,' I told Erimem.

She blinked and looked at me. 'That's is nice and thank you for the offer, but I am seeing someone.'

I swatted her arm. 'Not you, you tit. I want to get married to Olivia.'

'Oh.'

That wasn't the reaction I'd hoped for. 'Is that a good "oh" or a bad "oh", pal?'

'It is a surprised "oh", Andy,' she said, her face breaking into a wide smile, 'but a happy one. I take it Olivia has said yes?'

I scrunched my face up a bit. 'I'm not sure "said yes" was how I'd describe it.'

Her Queeniness nodded wisely. 'She shrieked?'

'You heard?'

Oh, she laughed then. A great big laugh. 'I think the entire city heard.' She sniffed primly. 'We thought you were simply having fun.'

'If I could get that kind of reaction from her in bed I'd be doing something very right.'

She tried for the disapproving look but her heart wasn't in it. 'Do you ever think of anything but sex?'

I gave that some thought. 'Occasionally I think about chips.'

She got a far away look in her eyes. 'Chips... I could never go back to Thebes permanently. No chips.'

'Me neither.' I studied her for a moment. I knew her well enough to know what was happening in her head. 'You're thinking about something. Spill the beans.'

'Just one thing...' she said softly. 'The Cleopatra rings...'

'Oh, god. What about them?'

She gave me a little smile. 'You are going to need wedding rings.'

Well, there's an offer for you. How was I to react to that. 'You're kidding.' Yeah, I'd have hoped for a better answer than that but she took me by surprise.

She was firm in her answer. 'No. I can think of no better way to use them. They are my gift to you both.'

What do you say when you're given the gift of wedding rings worth millions? I'm a hobby mare and I couldn't think of anything so I just hugged Erimem.

Okay, in the Covid world of 2020 how do you have a happy wedding? Well, you use time travel. You buzz around, working out what restrictions are in force at various times and you set it up so that you can get the maximum number of people there.

Hang on, some folks might say. Shouldn't Olivia be asked about this first?

Well, of course I talked to Olivia first. It would be a rubbish wedding if I was there all dolled up and looking lush and she was in a pair of leggings wandering round the local shopping centre desperately hoping to find somewhere open.

I was the most romantic me I could be. There were flowers, I had champagne, there was candle light… okay, that's all lies. I had been wracking my excuse for a brain for how to ask her. In the end I just blurted it out. We were in bed and I wasn't getting any sleep because this kept running through my head and so the words just fell out. I don't remember any of what I said but they must have worked because Robert is your auntie's husband, suddenly Olivia and me were getting hitched and picking engagement rings from the bits of treasure she'd liberated from her victims when she was a pirate. I picked diamonds, she went for sapphire.

There was much hugging and happiness at our little bombshell. Even Tom was genuinely pleased with the news. Nobody in our own little group was a problem. Nobody in 2020 was going to be a problem either. At least nobody with a functioning brain. The problem was that we don't live ordinary lives. Our friends are scattered through time and space. Rosa… I thought there was going to be some Catholic disapproval but that would be tempered by the fact that she liked us all. I was right. We told the Stones. They're our friends. Lisa was… surprised. Shocked, but she got over it pretty quick. Stone just shrugged and congratulated us. It wasn't the biggest surprise they were going to get.

The wedding took place outdoors at a country hotel. They were crippled for custom and so we hired the place. I did mention that we had gamed time travel so that we were utterly minted?

What nobody knew was that we had hired the place and, well, paid them to stay closed to everyone else for the weekend. In the grounds they had an archway through a wall. That was where Erimem placed the entrance to her Habitat. I had regrogrammed the interior. It was like having two desktops running on a PC. While Erimem's place ran on in one desktop, a beautiful sunny summer's day at a country hotel ran in the other. Nobody knew that they were in a totally different universe. They didn't know that as they went through the arch it deloused them for Covid either. Pity it couldn't do that for the world.

The celebrant was the happiest woman you've ever met. She just loved to see people in love and getting married. It still feels odd to talk about being "in love". It sounds so old school and 1950s, but it's how we feel and we're happy.

For a couple of days I'd laughed about my big gay wedding. Pretty quick, that changed. I just wanted people to call it my wedding. That lasted a few days and I slipped back into calling it various things, but at the heart, it was just my wedding.

I never thought I'd get married. Never even gave the idea a second of time. The more I thought about it and the closer it got, the more I knew it was the right thing.

Because we were playing silly buggers with time, other people had more time to get ready for it than we did. Orla, the Vice Chancellor at the University was incredibly excited and so pleased to be invited. We compressed our preparations into just a few days, and part of that time was spent buying houses. It sounds like we were rushing things, but I'm not sure we were. There was an intervention by everyone, asking about this, but… we just didn't see any point in waiting.

And they accepted that.

There were a few downsides from stupid people we hadn't even invited. A few stupid messages did come from people asking which one of us would wear the suit and which the dress, or who was the guy in bed. I swear this pandemic has brought some people's IQs even lower.

Fuck 'em. Fuck the whole lot of 'em.

This is our wedding and if they don't like any of it they can kiss my arse. Actually, no they can't. They can pucker up and French kiss each other's hoops. My butt is now off-limits.

That was our happy day and nobody was getting to spoil it.

And you know what? Nobody did.

Friends from the Uni like Trina, they were easy to deal with. To them it was just like going to the country hotel. Not a problem. Other friends, though… the ones with time to cross as well… yeah, they were a problem, but we got around it. Oh, god. You want to know how we got around it now, don't you? Okay, short version – time travel, moving the door to the Habitat, a lengthy road tunnel and a prodigious amount of spectacular fibbing. That was how we got Rosa, Laura and Stone and of course Duke to the wedding. He brought his wife. That was the decider that we'd have to involve a bit of amnesia, to be passed off as a howler of a hangover. Did we feel guilty about that? Well, yes, obviously we di... no. Not a bit. Not even a smidgette.

Everybody arrived, everybody sat in the sunshine and then... showtime.

To answer the balloons who asked which one of us wore a dress... we both did. Not frilly white lacy numbers. Nope. Olivia wore turquoise and I wore peach. Neither of us was walked down the aisle by a parent, but we were accompanied by a friend when we came from opposite sides of the table that was serving as an altar. Erimem was with me, Olivia had Helena at her side. No patriarchy here. No, ma'am.

I'm pretty sure Erimem and Helena looked amazing. I wasn't really paying attention to them.

I was just looking at Olivia.

And holy shit, we were getting married.

Because we'd hurried it had been quite an abstract idea. And then it got very real, very quickly, and I was just so happy. So was Olivia. And so was everybody else there. Well, Duke's wife looked pretty startled, so maybe she'd need an extra dose of amnesia. Duke? He got used to the idea pretty quick.

There was a lot of drinking a lot of eating, a lot of dancing (music ranging from 30s big bands to 70s disco tat, but nothing after that, thank you very much) and a lot of laughing.

And a few tears. I wish Mum and Dad could have been there. I even wished my brother could have been there but that's... that's a different story, a different world. Literally.

Mostly, it was just happy. I remember dancing slow. It was Eric Clapton, *Wonderful Tonight*. Normally I hate the song but gimme a break it was my wedding, okay? I was dancing with Olivia, and I saw Erimem dancing with Adam. She just gave me a silent look that said so much. She was happy for me and she was content for herself with this guy she'd found millennia after her birth. Helena danced with Ibrahim, Lisa with Stone and a lot of other couples were just together. I think even Tom brought a date. And I'm fairly sure Trina was making eyes at Duke after his wife went off to bed. He was a man of character. He will have declined.

It was just a happy day, and a day that happened because of the crazy, wonderful time-travelling life I had with my friends... my new family.

We were all happy.

Those were beautiful happy memories that would stay with us for a long time.

And we were going to need those happy memories, because the next time we gathered together formally it would be for a funeral and on that occasion, there would be nothing but tears.

Reviews

THE JEWELS OF CLEOPATRA
Dir: Lisa Stone

Cheapo adventure flick *Warrior Queen of the Nile* was an unexpected hit for low-budget experts Centurion, which led to a follow-up being rushed into production. Unlike most sequels, *The Jewels of Cleopatra* is an improvement on the first picture. It has a better script than you'd expect for this kind of quickie flick, unusually natural performances for 1940 and assured direction from first time director Lisa Stone (she won an Emmy in 1974 for *The Bridge Murders*). Possibly most unusual of all is finding a woman of color in the leading role without a hint of stereotyping to be seen. The action is well staged, with troops looking like they know what they're doing. The song and dance fight scene at the end is an unexpected delight. A little gem.

October 2015 review, **Hollywood Retrospective**

THE JEWELS OF CLEOPATRA (1940)
Screen Classics
Available for download from July 20th

You have to hand it to Centurion Pictures. When *Warrior Queen of the Nile* turned out to be a hit, they got the sequel in the theatres within eight months, and managed to make it an improvement on the predecessor.

Enigmatic Erimem Smith (one of the few Hollywood leading ladies of color, and one of whom almost nothing is known) is engaging and energetic as a sort of spectral protector of Egypt's history, flitting through time to deal with offences against the Pharaohs. Smith is known to have done her own stunts.

First film as director for Lisa Stone who would later win two Emmy Awards for a pair of classic noir TV movies.

A third film in the series, *The Power of Pharaoh*, followed in 1942.

Odd fact: The jewels used in the film were based on Cleopatra's own jewelry..

Rating ★★★☆☆
A solid three out of five.

2018 review, www.cheesymovies.ccdn

CENTURION STUDIOS
Autographed promotional
10 BY 8 glossy

STUDIO ANNOUNCEMENT

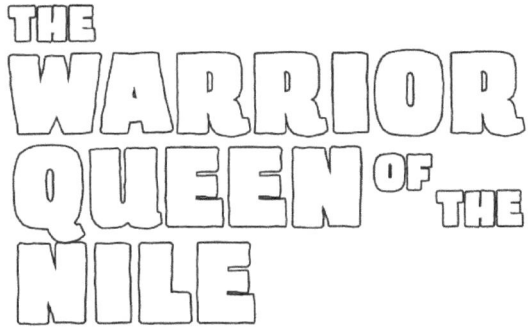

THE WARRIOR QUEEN OF THE NILE

WILL BE BACK IN

THE POWER OF PHARAOH

COMING 1942

A Centurion Picture

Coming soon from
THEBES PUBLISHING

SACRIFICE
A novel by Beth Jones

RETRIBUTION
A novel

A PHARAOH OF MARS
A novel by Jim Mortimore